Hidden Treasures of the

Heart

Donald Downing

To: Jim Penn
We Know The Heart is The
Key To Life Today And Eternally.
may This Book Bless You
In All Areas Of Life.
Bishop *Donald Downing*

Treasure House

An Imprint of

Destiny Image® Publishers, Inc.
P.O. Box 310
Shippensburg, PA 17257-0310

"For where your treasure is,
there will your heart be also." Matthew 6:21

ISBN 1-56043-315-9

For Worldwide Distribution
Printed in the U.S.A.

This book and all other Destiny Image, Revival Press, Mercy Place, Fresh Bread, and Treasure House books are available at Christian bookstores and distributors worldwide.

For a U.S. bookstore nearest you, call **1-800-722-6774.**
For more information on foreign distributors,
call **717-532-3040.**
Or reach us on the Internet: **http://www.reapernet.com**

Dedication
and
Acknowledgments

This book is dedicated to my precious Lord and Savior, Jesus Christ, who showed me His heart as He revealed to me my own heart's condition; who gave me the words to share; and who blessed and prospered me in the formation of this book...while He changed my heart! I give Him thanks and all praise and glory for being the true author of this book.

Also, to my lovely wife, Lezlie, and my daughter, Stephanie, who have faithfully stood by me in the ministry.

To the pastors of all the Free Gospel Churches, to Bishop Ralph E. Green, and to my family, who have shown me the meaning of true Christian love and worship.

To my very own dear congregation: thanks for your many prayers, your support, and your strength. Special thanks goes to my writer, Steve Nance, who understood my heart's tears and burden for this book. He opened his heart to make this book all that it is.

I thank you all from the bottom of my heart.

Contributors

I want to specifically thank those who have contributed both physical and spiritual labor to the birthing of this book:

Mrs. Hattie Broadnax
Mrs. Betty Carol
Mr. Anthony and Mrs. Karen Thomas
Mr. Lionel and Mrs. Linda Proctor
Mr. Michael and Mrs. Markette Lewis
Mr. Greg and Mrs. Recee Heyward
Miss Marchonie August
Dr. Bishop Ralph E. Green
Mrs. Noreen Battle
Lezlie and Stephanie Downing

Contents

Foreword:
Runaway Hearts

Where is the power to change a man from the evil passions of his heart? Does a power that could do such a thing even exist? The heart of man has been wicked for a long, long time. Philosophers and teachers throughout the centuries many times thought they had the ultimate solution. But time and human nature have proven them miserably wrong.

Even the prophet Jeremiah speaks with an apparent cruel finality when he says, "The heart is deceitful above all things, and desperately wicked: who can know it?" (Jer. 17:9) Who can know the heart of a man and who has the power to change what man cannot change himself?

From the dawn of history man has been plagued with a runaway heart. Out of control and beyond harnessing, the heart of man has left a legacy of pain, rampant greed, cold arrogance, and an insatiable lust for power. In flagrant disobedience to his God, the heart of man sought equality with his Maker in the Garden, slew his brother Abel, built a tower to reach God, crucified His only Son, and to this day, defies the tenderness of God's gentle wooing.

Throughout the ages the prophets have warned, pleaded with, and condemned the wanton arrogance lodged within humanity. David decries the fool who says from his heart, "There is no God" (Ps. 14:1). Jeremiah pleads with a rebellious humanity who "walks in the imagination of their own hearts" to "wash your heart from evil" (Jer. 4:14; 23:17). Hosea saw the heart of man "set on iniquity" (see Hos. 4:8). No wonder Joel cries out, "Rend your heart, and not your garments" (Joel 2:13). At least Joel saw hope. If man could rend his heart, he could change. If man could tear away at the stiff-necked self-determination of his heart, God's love just might find a home there.

God, too, sees the same possibility in man that Joel did, for in spite of the wandering of man's heart, God does not cease to draw us to Himself. For He has prepared a remedy for the failing and hopeless heart of man. He has prepared the Blood of Jesus, whose power is the hope for our desperate need. He has provided a means through which the heart can be cleansed, healed, and prepared to respond to the purpose of God instead of our hopeless gratification.

We can trust in a renewed heart, for the Lord Himself is He who renews. The Lord Jesus has rent His heart for us. He has created the possibilities that at one time were thought impossible. He has made our hearts changeable, flexible, patient, compassionate, loving and merciful.

Now everything that God has created us to be can come to pass. Now those around us can feel the love of God and experience His attributes through us. Now the Person and the Presence of the Lord is brought closer to a needy humanity because His Life is being released in us. Yes, the Word is becoming flesh—in you and I. All the possibilities within you can now be seen.

When the Lord formed you in your mother's womb, when you were fearfully and wonderfully made, He had a marvelous plan. In the deepest fibers of your heart, He wove the greatest possibilities that a man or woman could hope for. Now, by the Blood of Jesus, through the power of the rent veil, you are free to love, care, nurture, encourage, and grow to the fullest of the dream He has dreamed for you, both for your sake, and for those you love.

Don Nori, Sr.
Founder, CEO, Destiny Image Publishers

Introduction

One of the keys to God's Kingdom is knowledge; not the knowledge gotten through a worldly education, but the revelation knowledge that God imparts to His children. Lack of this divine, spiritual knowledge is deadly:

> *My people are destroyed for lack of knowledge: because thou hast rejected knowledge, I will also reject thee, that thou shalt be no priest to Me: seeing thou hast forgotten the law of thy God, I will also forget thy children* (Hosea 4:6).

This knowledge is so critical that Jesus harshly criticized the Jewish teachers of the law for denying it to the people:

> *Woe unto you, lawyers! for ye have taken away the key of knowledge: ye entered not in yourselves, and them that were entering in ye hindered* (Luke 11:52).

Second Peter 3:9 says that God is not willing that any should perish but that everyone should come to repentance, and First Timothy 2:4 avows that God desires "all men to be saved, and to come unto the knowledge of the truth."

Spiritual knowledge is important. In fact, it is critical for our life and our future.

One morning in 1985 during my daily meditation time, God broke through my commonsense knowledge and changed the course of my ministry. At that time I had been a Christian for about four years and, by God's grace, had come through some severe trials and tribulations. The Lord had also blessed me with a teaching ministry that focused on the works, sacrifice, blood, and redemption of Jesus Christ.

That morning a small voice broke through the stillness of my meditation and spoke into my spirit: "Not everyone knows who Jesus is." That was all. Although it seemed strange to me to hear such a voice, I nevertheless agreed with what it said. I did nothing about it, however, and a week later the same voice came again during my meditation time: "Not everyone knows who Jesus is." This time I responded: "They sure don't know!" Then the voice spoke to me with clear authority: "*You* don't know who I am!"

That revelation disturbed me. I determined then to learn as much about the Lord as I could. I searched the Bible, studied commentaries, questioned church elders; I did everything I could think of to increase my knowledge. I was encouraged by Matthew 11:29: "Take My yoke upon you, and learn of Me; for I am meek and lowly in heart: and ye shall find rest unto your souls."

Over several months of intense study I discovered that the Bible contains over 365 names and titles for Jesus—enough to call upon Him with a different name each day of the year! I began to teach on the wonderful names and titles of the Lord. I taught about the power, the benefits, the authority, the purpose, and the meaning of the names of Jesus. I taught how and when to use the mighty names of Jesus.

Then one day, during my time of meditation on the Word, the Lord spoke to me again: "Not everyone knows what love is. It doesn't do them any good to know who I am and not love Me. My will is for all of mankind not just to know My name, but also to love Me as I have loved them!" I envisioned thousands of Christians possessing head knowledge of the names of Jesus but with little knowledge of how to love Him or each other. Before long, I realized that many, many people don't even understand the true meaning of the word *love*. In fact, *I* didn't even understand it!

Again, I searched the Scriptures diligently and scoured commentaries and other study aids to learn what God's love is. I discovered that there are many types of love, but without *agape*, the God-kind of love, there can be no salvation and no one can be a disciple of Christ. Without *agape* there is no healing, no forgiveness, and no covering for our sins.

I realized how many faith, healing, deliverance, preaching, and teaching ministries there were across the country, yet how few ministries there were that focused on love. I was not aware of any that were devoted to preaching and teaching how to develop, abide in, and demonstrate the love of Jesus Christ. Convinced that love was the final answer, I began to teach it and preach it, from the Philippines to Korea; from Tulsa, Oklahoma, to Washington, D.C.

Yet God had still another turn for my ministry. In 1988 He spoke to me once more. You would think that by this time I would easily recognize His voice. However, as entrenched as I was in my conviction that love is the ultimate thing, I was unprepared to hear Him say: "There is something greater, something more important than love."

I am embarrassed to admit that my first reaction to this word was to deny it. I said, "I rebuke you, devil!" God, in His infinite love, grace, and patience, simply said, "Don, I will reveal it to you and then you will have ears to hear." At that time my carnal mind could not receive His revelation.

For several months I had no further personal lessons from the Lord. Then one day while I was driving, the voice of God broke into my thoughts once again: "Don, you say that I live inside of you. Where do I live?"

"Why, within my heart, Lord," I answered.

A few miles further on He spoke again: "Where does my Word dwell? Where do faith, love, joy, peace, and truth dwell?"

I felt a chill rush through my body. "Lord," I cried out, "they all dwell in my heart!" At that moment I realized that there is something more important than love: the heart, the place where God's love dwells in man! As thrilling as this realization was for me, it was the Lord's next statement that drastically changed my life.

"Don," He said, "your heart is not right with Me!"

I stopped the car by the side of the road and for the next 15 minutes simply stared at the windshield as God exposed to me the true condition of my heart. Everything rushed up so fast that my mind was reeling. I suddenly understood that everything concerning the Kingdom of God on earth—love, joy, faith, healing, salvation—is administered and transmitted to a dying world from the *heart* of God's people. I saw that the heart is God's seat of operation within humans and that my "heartquarters" was not ready for my Master's use.

During the weeks that followed I was drawn to much confession, repentance, and prayer as God continued to reveal to me more and more of my personal errors and the errors of the Church as a whole with regard to matters of the heart. He showed me that many, many Christians do not really understand that the only sacrifice, service, and worship that God can accept is that which comes from the heart. It is as Isaiah wrote (see also Mt. 15:7-9):

Wherefore the Lord said, Forasmuch as this people draw near Me with their mouth, and with their lips do honour Me, but have removed their heart far from Me, and their fear toward Me is taught by the precept of men: therefore, behold, I will proceed to do a marvellous work among this people, even a marvellous work and a wonder: for the wisdom of their wise men shall perish,

*and the understanding of their prudent men shall be
hid* (Isaiah 29:13-14).

In light of this revelation I began to examine my spiritual
heart. Like King David, I asked God to change my motives
and to "create in me a clean heart" (see Ps. 51:10). I prayed
that the meditations of my heart might be acceptable in His
sight. I petitioned the Lord for a "heart-to-heart" walk with
Him. By His grace God began to raise my spirit man above
my natural desires. My heart knowledge began to take prece-
dence over my head knowledge and my past experiences. My
carnal thoughts and imaginations were cast down by the
Word of God in my heart. I began to harness my tongue to
speak only "what is written" out of the abundance of my
heart. Now, as I meditate on the Word of God, my prayer is
"Lord, Thy Word have I hid in mine heart, that I might not
sin against Thee" (see Ps. 119:11).

Of course, I am far from perfect and make many, many
mistakes, but the Lord is teaching me to look to my heart, as
He does. That's the lesson we all must learn. For so long,
much of my personal holiness was in my head and not in my
heart. So much of my ministry had been developed according
to the precepts of men rather than by the spiritual revelation
of God.

*But the Lord said unto Samuel, Look not on his coun-
tenance, or on the height of his stature; because I have
refused him: for the Lord seeth not as man seeth; for
man looketh on the outward appearance, **but the Lord
looketh on the heart*** (1 Samuel 16:7).

Who we are in our heart is, in the final analysis, all that the
Spirit of God really "knows" about us. If our heart is far from
God, how *can* He "know" us? In a sense, sin is no longer
man's greatest enemy. Jesus took care of sin on the cross. All
we must do is repent and put our faith and trust in Him, and
our sins are forgiven. The real enemy of our dying world and

the sleeping Church is our rebellious, disobedient, unbelieving, hardened heart. Jesus died to forgive our sins, yet it is our *heart* that can keep us from believing and repenting and turning to Jesus in faith to receive forgiveness.

Keep thy heart with all diligence; for out of it are the issues of life (Proverbs 4:23).

We need to understand the critical importance of the heart to our spiritual health and well-being. We also need to be aware of the critically ill condition of the heart of many in the Church as well as the world. God looks at our heart; we must do likewise. We must learn to give attention to our inner spirit man, what Peter calls the "hidden man of the heart" (see 1 Pet. 3:4). We must learn to examine our heart and make sure it is right before God. We must learn to recognize what is hidden in our heart, be it treasure or trash. That's the purpose of this book.

Prologue:
Hidden Treasures
of the Heart

We stand on the brink of a new millennium in a world that is bursting with knowledge. Every day new discoveries are made in the fields of science and medicine. The sum total of man's knowledge is now doubling every 5 to 10 years. Due to the Internet and the World-Wide Web, as well as the broadcast and print media, never before has so much knowledge and information been so readily available to so many people so quickly as today.

At the same time, never has mankind as a whole been so ignorant and deceived concerning our true nature. Science can explore the mind and study the brain, and medicine can discover new and better ways to heal the body, but neither can do anything about the *heart* of man, the inner *spiritual* person that represents the core of who we *really* are. In First Peter 3:4 Peter calls this inner person the "hidden man of the heart."

Very few people know who they really are. The *true* nature of our heart is concealed from most of us. Our sin separates us from God and dulls our awareness to the reality that we are sinners. The world offers outwardly attractive alternatives that promise happiness and fulfillment but lead only to heartache and failure: sex, drugs, money, possessions, pleasure, knowledge, New Age and other man-centered philosophies—you name it. Satan blinds us to the reality of our true condition and deceives us by tempting us to focus on external factors that ignore the spirit man. In addition, satan also deceives us with regard to the true nature of God, casting doubt into our mind about God's love for us and His fairness toward us.

For these reasons as well as others, most people do not know the true condition of their heart. God does, however. The Bible makes this very plain: "The heart is deceitful above all things, and desperately wicked: who can know it? I the Lord search the heart, I try the reins, even to give every man according to his ways, and according to the fruit of his doings" (Jer. 17:9-10), and "Shall not God search this out? for He knoweth the secrets of the heart" (Ps. 44:21). If we are to know the true condition of our heart, if we are to understand the secrets of our inner nature, we must look to God who alone knows everything there is to know about us and who can reveal these things to us.

Unfortunately, this ignorance of the true nature of the inner man is a problem for church people too. Many believers do not know their own heart. They live frustrated and defeated lives, failing to be all that God wants them to be, because of hidden areas, the secret places in their heart where sin, wickedness, unbelief, and rebellion dwell. In a similar manner, there are others in the church who believe that they are saved when they are not because they have never truly given their heart to God. The problem is, they don't know this.

The secret to true success in life is to unlock the secret places of our heart so that we may truly know what is hidden whether treasure or trash is hidden there. Only then can we truly surrender our heart to God. This means that we refuse to trust in our own heart, which is "deceitful above all things," but rather learn to rest and abide in the secret places of God, persuaded that we are fully hidden in Christ Jesus and covered by His blood. True success does not mean having millions of dollars or a popular name, but rather having the hidden things of God in full operation in our heart. Love, joy, peace, truth, righteousness, holiness—these are the treasures we should seek and value.

God gives from Himself and of Himself to our spirit man in secret so that we may manifest Him openly in the earth. The Holy Spirit works in the heart of God's children to reveal in us His glory, His attributes, and His mighty power so that we may succeed in all that He requires of us and attain true victory. Our victory depends on the condition of our heart in Christ Jesus. We must embrace the love of God, our faith in Christ, and our confidence in the Word of God from a pure and clean heart.

How can we know our heart's condition—whether it contains treasure or trash? How do we unlock the secret places of our heart and present to God a heart that is clean and pure? The answer is quite simple. God has given us two important keys: His Word and prayer. God's Word can reveal the innermost secrets of our heart: "For the word of God is quick, and powerful, and sharper than any twoedged sword, piercing even to the dividing asunder of soul and spirit, and of the joints and marrow, and is a discerner of the thoughts and intents of the heart" (Heb. 4:12). Prayer, on the other hand, can change our heart, for God has promised to answer prayer lifted up in His name: "Ask, and it shall be given you; seek, and ye shall find; knock, and it shall be opened unto you: for every one that asketh receiveth; and he that seeketh findeth; and to him that knocketh it shall be opened" (Mt. 7:7-8), and "If any of you lack wisdom, let him ask of God, that giveth to all men liberally, and upbraideth not; and it shall be given him" (Jas. 1:5).

This book reveals additional keys, which, when used with the keys of prayer and the Word, will reveal the treasures of a heart that is pleasing to God and worthy before men. The first key unlocks the door to understanding the critically ill condition of the heart of man. This is where we all must begin. The second key opens the door that reveals God's health care plan for the human heart. Man's heart is critically ill, what is God doing about it?

In addition to these, there are keys that release understanding of the qualities of a God-pleasing heart: faith, purity, love, joy, peace, power, faithfulness, and victory.

Only God can unlock the secrets and hidden treasures of the heart. He has given us the keys in His Word. Let us explore together the inner chambers of our heart, unlocking each door as we come to it. At the end of the journey we will know our heart and will understand how to present it to God, clean, pure, healthy, renewed, and forgiven—a heart and life that are pleasing to Him.

Chapter 1

Knowing Your Heart's Condition

The heart is deceitful above all things, and desperately wicked: who can know it? (Jeremiah 17:9)

"My heart! Oh, my heart!

The man clutched at his chest and fell to the ground, his face blue, his eyes full of pain and fear. Every effort was made to resuscitate him: CPR, defibrillation, drugs; all to no avail. His life rapidly slipped away. In a matter of minutes he was gone.

Scenarios similar to this occur by the hundreds every day in homes, offices, ambulances, and hospital emergency rooms all across the country. In fact, cardiovascular diseases—heart attacks, strokes, congestive heart failure, and the like—account for nearly half of all deaths in the industrialized world. Whether caused by congenital defects, an unhealthy lifestyle, or the stresses of modern life, heart problems are a major concern for many people. Indeed, heart health is central to quality of life.

Every year billions of dollars are spent on medical and scientific research in the treatment and cure of heart disease. Consumers spend millions more on diet and fitness plans, health club memberships, and exercise equipment in an effort to make and keep their heart healthy. Although this concern for physical health and fitness is good, there is a more serious problem.

Spiritual Heart Problems

The human race has a deadly heart condition. It affects everyone: men, women, and children. No one is immune. Left untreated, it is 100 percent fatal. There are no drugs, no treatments, no therapy of men that will cure this problem. It is beyond the reach of medical science. I'm talking about a *spiritual* heart disorder, a malady that afflicts the spirit man—the innermost self—of every person on earth.

A physical heart attack occurs when there is an insufficient supply of blood to the heart. Typically this is caused by a blood clot or some other blockage in one or more of the coronary arteries that provide a steady flow of blood to the heart. Adequate blood flow is critical for life. If we lose too much blood through a wound, we will die. If the flow of blood through our body ceases, we will die. The heart, which pumps blood throughout our body, itself needs blood to stay alive and to function properly. Scripture says, "For the life of the flesh is in the blood" (Lev. 17:11a). We need blood to survive.

Treatment for heart attacks includes the use of thrombolytics—anti-clotting drugs that thin the blood—and angioplasty, where a balloon is inflated in the blocked artery in order to open it up. More serious cases require bypass surgery, where blood vessels from the legs are grafted onto the heart to bypass the blocked coronary arteries. The aim of all these treatments is to *restore* and *maintain* the flow of life-giving blood to the heart and the rest of the body.

Sometimes a person's heart becomes so weakened and damaged that it cannot be restored. For many people in this situation, the modern medical miracle of a heart transplant offers hope. Since the first one was conducted in the 1960's, heart transplants have become commonplace, giving hundreds of cardiac patients a new lease on life.

In a similar way the spiritual heart disorder that affects every person on earth obstructs and blocks the flow of spiritual life from God to the spirit man, the inner person that defines who we *really* are, as opposed to the outer person that we put on display for other people. Because of the sin of Adam and Eve in the Garden of Eden, every person is born with a congenital disorder of the spiritual heart. King David wrote that we were conceived in sin and "shapen in iniquity" (Ps. 51:5). "Iniquity" translates the Hebrew word *avon*, which means "perversity" or "moral evil." *Avon* comes from the Hebrew root *avah*, which means to "make crooked," "to pervert," or "to do wickedly."[1]

Each of us was born with a sick, wicked spiritual heart that is perverse and bent toward moral evil. We have inherited a heart that is self-willed and rebellious, corrupted by the pride and arrogance of satan who deceived Adam and Eve with the sin that was born in his own heart:

> How art thou fallen from heaven, O Lucifer, son of the morning! how art thou cut down to the ground, which didst weaken the nations! For thou hast said in thine heart, I will ascend into heaven, I will exalt my throne above the stars of God...I will ascend above the heights of the clouds; I will be like the most High (Isaiah 14:12-14).

Satan conceived in his heart (his inmost being) the desire to seize the throne of Heaven and depose God. Adam and Eve were infected by sin when they were deceived and listened to satan's lies in the garden. That infection has been passed to every succeeding generation of the human family. Our spiritual heart is so critically ill that it cannot be restored. The only solution is a heart transplant. If we hope to survive, then we must receive a *new* heart: a heart that is free of the disease and corruption of sin and wickedness.

The Hidden Man of the Heart

In practical terms the world generally shows little regard for the spiritual side of life. Science and medicine are devoted almost exclusively to the physical, mental, and emotional realms of human experience. Many of the problems that appear in these areas are symptoms of an underlying spiritual sickness that more often than not is virtually ignored.

The Bible, however, does not ignore it. Scripture clearly reveals a spiritual side of us that is more significant even than our natural side. The apostle Peter wrote:

> But let it be the **hidden man of the heart**, in that which is not corruptible, even the ornament of a meek and quiet spirit, which is in the sight of God of great price (1 Peter 3:4).

This "hidden man of the heart" is not a visible, flesh and blood human being, but a spiritual man brought to life in our spiritual heart as a result of the new birth that Jesus spoke of:

> ...Except a man be born again, he cannot see the kingdom of God....Except a man be born of water and of the Spirit, he cannot enter into the kingdom of God. That which is born of the flesh is flesh; and that which is born of the Spirit is spirit. Marvel not that I said unto thee, Ye must be born again (John 3:3,5b-7).

In the Greek, the phrase *born again* literally means "born from above." It refers to a spiritual process that is accomplished outside of any human method or agency. To be "born from above" means to be "born of the Spirit [of God]." There is a "spirit man" in each of us that must be given birth to if we are to "see the kingdom of God."

The apostle Paul referred to this "hidden man of the heart" as a completely new creation:

Therefore if any man be in Christ, he is a new creature: old things are passed away; behold, all things are become new (2 Corinthians 5:17).

When he wrote to the Corinthians regarding the resurrection of the dead, Paul made a clear distinction between the natural and the spiritual:

So also is the resurrection of the dead. It is sown in corruption; it is raised in incorruption: it is sown in dishonour; it is raised in glory: it is sown in weakness; it is raised in power: it is sown a natural body; it is raised a spiritual body. There is a natural body, and there is a spiritual body (1 Corinthians 15:42-44).

According to Peter the hidden man of the heart is "that which is not corruptible." Paul says that the spirit man will be "raised incorruptible" (1 Cor. 15:52). This is in direct contrast to the congenitally "corrupt" nature of the sinful and rebellious heart we inherited from Adam and Eve.

The hidden man of the heart is our innermost self, the part of us that communicates with, relates to, and fellowships with God. This inner spiritual man has eyes and ears. When God speaks to us, He speaks to our hidden man of the heart. In Romans 8:16 Paul says that God's Spirit bears witness with our spirit. Jesus said, "It is the *spirit* that *quickeneth*; the flesh profiteth nothing: *the words that I speak* unto you, *they are spirit, and they are life*" (Jn. 6:63). Often Jesus concluded His parables with the words, "He that hath ears to hear, let him hear" (e.g. Mt. 11:15), referring to the spiritual ears of the hidden man of the heart. Jesus' truth was intended for the spiritual man. In fact, only the spiritual man can understand spiritual truth. Paul made this clear when he wrote:

> *But the natural man receiveth not the things of the Spir-*
> *it of God: for they are foolishness unto him: neither can*
> *he know them, because they are spiritually discerned.*
> *But he that is spiritual judgeth all things, yet he himself*
> *is judged of no man. For who hath known the mind of*
> *the Lord, that he may instruct Him? But we have the*
> *mind of Christ* (1 Corinthians 2:14-16).

The Heart in the Word

The Bible refers to the heart over 1,000 times. In the Old Testament, the Hebrew word *leb* and its synonym *lebab* occur 860 times.[2] In the strictest sense these words refer to the physical organ that pumps blood through the body. In a much broader sense they are used to describe characteristics that make up the center or core of man's being. The "heart" refers to the inner man as opposed to the outer man. It is the seat of desire, will, emotion, knowledge, wisdom, conscience, and moral character. It is also the seat of pride and rebellion.[3] In short, "The 'heart' stands for the inner being of man, the man himself. As such, it is the fountain of all he does (Prov. 4:4). All his thoughts, desires, words, and actions flow from deep within him."[4]

In the New Testament, the Greek word for "heart," *kardia*, occurs 161 times. In addition to being the word for the physical heart (our word *cardiac* is derived from it), *kardia* also came to mean "man's entire mental and moral activity, both the rational and the emotional elements."[5] The Bible regards the "heart" of man as both the seat of human depravity that influences and defiles all our actions and the sphere of divine influence through which God speaks to us.[6]

Clearly, then, when the Bible speaks of the "heart" of man, it is referring to much more than a fist-sized muscle that pumps blood through the body. The "heart" of man is the center, the core, the essence of his being; it is his innermost self, the totality of his nature, desires, emotions, thoughts, and actions.

The Heart of Man

What is our heart condition? How does the Bible describe the heart of man? What's the diagnosis of the Word of God? It's quite bad, I'm afraid; it's terminal, in fact. Scripture makes it clear that humankind, every one of us, suffers from *spiritual heart failure*. Let's look at some examples.

The first occurrence of the word *heart* in Scripture is in chapter 6 of Genesis, where we find that the evil nature of men's heart, and not sin alone, was the primary reason for the Flood:

> *And God saw that the wickedness of man was great in the earth, and that every* **imagination of the thoughts of his heart was only evil continually**. *And it repented the Lord that He had made man on the earth, and it grieved Him at His heart. And the Lord said, I will destroy man whom I have created from the face of the earth; both man, and beast, and the creeping thing, and the fowls of the air; for it repenteth Me that I have made them* (Genesis 6:5-7).

"Imagination" is a translation of the Hebrew word *yetser*, which also means "conception," "purpose," or "work."[7] "Thoughts" translates the Hebrew word *machashabah*, which means "a contrivance," "intention," "plan," or "purpose."[8] Man was totally corrupt in his heart; he was corrupt in everything he thought, planned, or did. He thought about sin, he planned sin, and by this he did sin. His (man's) heart was not right in the sight of God.[9]

Later, after the Flood in which God preserved Noah and his family and following which He has promised that He would never again destroy all living things, God nevertheless acknowledges that "the imagination of *man's heart is evil* from his youth" (Gen. 8:21b). Noah, a man who had "found grace in the eyes of the Lord" and who "walked with God" (see Gen. 6:8-9), nonetheless suffered from the same spiritual heart disease as those who had died in the Flood. Like all people of every generation since Adam and Eve, Noah inherited a wicked heart.

The Book of Ecclesiastes tells us that "the heart of the sons of men is full of evil, and madness is in their heart while they live" (Eccles. 9:3b). We learn in the Book of Proverbs that "as he [man] thinketh in his heart, so is he" (Prov. 23:7a) and that we should *"Keep [our] heart with all diligence; for out of it are the issues of life"* (Prov. 4:23). Little wonder, then, that our world is plagued with the evil and madness that has issued forth from human hearts that are sick and festering with wickedness!

God did not mince any words when He gave His assessment of the human heart condition to the prophet Jeremiah: "The heart is deceitful above all things, and desperately wicked: who can know it?" (Jer. 17:9) The Hebrew word for "deceitful" is *aqob*, which also means "fraudulent," "crooked," and "polluted."[10] "Desperately wicked" translates the Hebrew *anash*, which also means "frail," "feeble," and "incurable."[11]

> Jesus said, *But those things which proceed out of the mouth come forth from the heart; and they defile the man. For out of the heart proceed evil thoughts, murders, adulteries, fornications, thefts, false witness, blasphemies: these are the things which defile a man* (Matthew 15:18-20a),

and the apostle Paul wrote to the Galatians:

> *Now the works of the flesh* [which issue forth from the heart] *are manifest, which are these; adultery, fornication, uncleanness, lasciviousness, idolatry, witchcraft,*

hatred, variance, emulations, wrath, strife, seditions, heresies, envyings, murders, drunkenness, revellings, and such like: of the which I tell you before, as I have also told you in time past, that they which do such things shall not inherit the kingdom of God (Galatians 5:19-21).

Make no mistake about it. The entire human race is sick unto death from spiritual heart failure. The heart of man is desperately, incurably diseased from the corrupting pollution of sin, wickedness, and evil imaginations. What a contrast to the spotless heart of God!

The Heart of God

God is good. In the beginning, God created all things and found His creation to be "good" (see Gen. 1). After the creation of man God surveyed everything He had made and pronounced it "very good" (Gen. 1:31). God's creation was good because God Himself is good. Everything that issues forth from God is good. It can be no other way. Everything that God says or does is an expression of His very nature, or His *heart*. Absolute goodness issues forth from the heart of God.

God is holy. He commanded the Israelites: "For I am the Lord your God: ye shall therefore sanctify yourselves, and ye shall be holy; for I am holy" (Lev. 11:44a). To say that God is holy is to say that He is absolutely pure without any spot or shadow of uncleanness; He is free of moral imperfection of any kind. Holiness is an expression of the heart of God.

God is love. Love issues forth from the heart of God. The apostle John wrote, "Beloved, let us love one another: for *love is of God*; and every one that loveth is born of God, and knoweth God. He that loveth not knoweth not God; for *God is love*" (1 Jn. 4:7-8). Every expression of God toward man is an expression of His love. The greatest expression of His love was Jesus: "For *God so loved the world*, that He gave His only begotten Son, that whosoever believeth in Him should not perish, but have everlasting life" (Jn. 3:16).

If God is love, then His Spirit is the Spirit of love. Paul described to the Galatians some of the qualities that are in the heart of God: "But the fruit of the Spirit is love, joy, peace, longsuffering, kindness, goodness, faithfulness, gentleness, self-control. Against such there is no law" (Gal. 5:22-23 NKJ). That's quite a contrast to the earlier list of the "works of the flesh"!

The heart of God is to bless all people and for all people to know Him and love Him:

> *For I know the thoughts that I think toward you, says the Lord, thoughts of peace and not of evil, to give you a future and a hope. Then you will call upon Me and go and pray to Me, and I will listen to you. And you will seek Me and find Me, when you search for Me with all your heart. I will be found by you, says the Lord...* (Jeremiah 29:11-14 NKJ).

Man was created in the image and likeness of God. He made us to be reflections of His heart; to reflect goodness, holiness, love, joy, peace, longsuffering, kindness, faithfulness, gentleness, and self-control. Why is it then that we do not reflect the heart of the God who made us in His image? Our sinfulness, evil, and wickedness have blocked the flow of the life-giving Spirit to us and we have suffered spiritual heart failure. It is terminal and there is no cure. Our only hope is to receive a new heart. We need a spiritual heart transplant. Fortunately for us, God has a solution. We need to make sure we are covered under *God's heart protection plan.*

Endnotes

1. James Strong, *Strong's Exhaustive Concordance of the Bible* (Peabody, MA: Hendrickson Publishers, n.d., #H5771 and #H5753.
2. W.E. Vine, Merrill F. Unger and William White, Jr. *Vine's Complete Expository Dictionary of Old and New Testament Words* (Nashville: Thomas Nelson Publishers, 1985), p. 108.
3. *Vine's*, pp. 108-10.
4. *Vine's*, p. 109.
5. *Vine's*, p. 297.
6. *Vine's*, p. 297.
7. *Strong's*, #H3336.
8. *Strong's*, #H4284.
9. Please note that the term *man* automatically includes the woman (female) also.
10. *Strong's*, #H6121.
11. *Strong's*, #H605.

Chapter 2

God's Health Plan for Your Heart

*Therefore if any man be in Christ, he is **a new creature**: old things are passed away; behold, all things are become new* (2 Corinthians 5:17).

*For in Christ Jesus neither circumcision availeth any thing, nor uncircumcision, but **a new creature*** (Galatians 6:15).

Whenever you get ready to buy an insurance policy or a health care plan, there are several things you need to consider. First, what does the plan cover? How comprehensive is it? In other words, what are the benefits of the plan? What will you get for your money? Second, is the plan right for you? Will it meet the specific needs of your particular circumstances? Third, how much will the plan cost? Can you afford the payments? Will the plan fit into your budget? Fourth, what is the reputation of the company offering the plan? Is it financially sound? Does it have a good record of serving the needs of its clients? Can it be trusted to honor the terms of your policy? Is it known for honesty and integrity?

As members of the human race, every one of us is in desperate need of spiritual health care. Our hearts are terminally ill and need to be replaced. We need a spiritual heart transplant, a "change of heart." God offers us a "heart protection plan" designed to give us that change of heart. What are the benefits? God's plan covers everything needed for transplant and recovery and for the growth and development of a strong, healthy heart. Is it the right plan? you ask. It is the *only* plan. There is no other option for dealing with our heart problem. How much does it cost? God has already paid the premium in full. Although it cost Him the life of His only Son, God offers His plan to us *free of charge*. All we have to do is turn over to Him our *old* heart—which is as good as dead anyway—in exchange for the new one He will give us. Can He be trusted? He is God, whose Word is truth, whose promises never fail, and whose riches and resources encompass all of creation. Yes, God can be trusted.

A New Heart

Nothing takes God by surprise. He was not caught unawares by the sin of Adam and Eve in the Garden of Eden. Even before He created them He knew that they would be deceived by the devil's lies and that their heart would become proud and corrupt, just as satan's was. God put His heart protection plan for man into action before the foundation of the world. (See Revelation 13:8; see also John 17:24; Ephesians 1:4; Hebrew 4:3; and First Peter 1:19-20.)

In the beginning, "God created man in His own image, in the image of God created He him; male and female created He them" (Gen. 1:27). "Image" in this verse is the Hebrew word *tselem*, which also means "resemblance" or a "representative figure."[1] Interestingly, it is the same word used in the second commandment: "Thou shalt not make unto thee any graven *image...*" (Ex. 20:4). Man was created to resemble God, to display His attributes and character, and to share His heart and nature. He was formed from the dust of the earth to rule, guide, and govern the earth and all its creatures. The divine purpose for man was that he would walk with God, being forever in God's presence and glory and sharing in God's divine knowledge. Adam could think, reason, and enjoyed constant, open fellowship with God. On the earth he was a little "god" made in the likeness of the Almighty God of Heaven.

From the outset, man was created to find his completeness and fulfillment in communion with God. Man was never designed to be outside of God's will, God's Word, or God's presence. Perfect fellowship, perfect unity, perfect relationship— these were God's intentions at creation. When God saw that it was "not good that the man should be alone," He made Adam a "help meet for him" (Gen. 2:18). The New King James translation renders that last phrase as "a helper comparable to him." At first, Adam and Eve walked with God in innocence, peace, and joy with a pure and holy heart. They enjoyed perfect harmony with God and with each other. There was completeness. The unity between the man and the woman was so complete in fact that Adam exclaimed of her, "This is now bone of my bones, and flesh of my flesh" (Gen. 2:23a).

The harmony and innocence in the garden of Eden did not last long. Satan, that fallen angel who desired to rule the earth as his domain, tempted Adam and Eve. Deceived by satan's lies, they chose to disobey God. The consequences were instantaneous and catastrophic. Through their sin Adam and Eve gave God's archenemy the rights to every one of earth's systems, including man's. Satan became the "god of this world" (2 Cor. 4:4). Adam and Eve died spiritually, their heart poisoned from within.[2] God pronounced the judgment of death upon them and, because unrighteousness and righteousness cannot dwell together, cast them out of the garden of His presence.

Yet even as God pronounced judgment on man's sin, He issued words of hope. Addressing the serpent, the Lord said, "And I will put enmity between thee and the woman, and between thy seed and *her seed; it shall bruise thy head*, and thou shalt bruise his heel" (Gen. 3:15). It is generally accepted that the woman's seed that would bruise the serpent's head is an early reference to Jesus. God had already put His heart protection plan into action!

Each of us must receive a new heart if we are to be right with God. God wants us to have a new heart so that we may be right with Him. He makes this clear in the Bible. First, God *promises* to give us a new heart:

> *A new heart also will I give you, and a new spirit will I put within you: and I will take away the stony heart out of your flesh, and I will give you an heart of flesh. And I will put My spirit within you, and cause you to walk in My statutes, and ye shall keep My judgments, and do them* (Ezekiel 36:26-27).

The word *flesh* is translated from the Hebrew word *basar*, which comes from a root that means "fresh." By extension, the word also means "body" or "person."[3] It can also mean "life itself."[4] In this context we should understand that God will take away from us the stone-cold, hard, and dead heart of sin and give us a fresh new heart full of life and vibrancy. The word for "spirit" in Hebrew is *ruwach*, which also means "breath" or "wind" and, in a figurative sense, can also mean "life."[5] God will take out of us the old, dead, stony heart and give us His Spirit, His life, His heart.

Secondly, God *commands* us to receive a new heart:

> *That ye **put off** concerning the former conversation **the old man** [heart], which is corrupt according to the deceitful lusts; and be renewed in the spirit of your*

*mind; and that ye **put on the new man** [heart], which after God is created in righteousness and true holiness* (Ephesians 4:22-24).

The condition of the heart determines the condition of the man. Look at the contrast. The old man (heart) is corrupt, deceitful, and lustful. The new man (heart) is righteous and holy. This new man is the "hidden man of the heart."

Now that we have a new heart, it must be protected...by the faith of God, the love of God, and the Word of God. The guarantee for God's heart protection plan was the death and resurrection of Jesus. Christ died that we might live. He gave His heart in death that we might receive His heart in new life. This was the "heart" of God's plan, ordained before time and unfolded through the ages so that it came to pass in the fullness of time.

Protected by the Law

Before Christ came there was the Law. God made for Himself a people through whom He desired to extend His heart protection plan to all the nations. He chose Abraham; called him out of his home, family, and country; and made a covenant with him to bless him and make of him a great nation. From Abraham descended Jacob and his sons, whose offspring grew to a great multitude in Egypt and suffered centuries of slavery at the hands of the Egyptians. Under God's leadership Moses delivered the Hebrew people from the Egyptians and led them to Mt. Sinai, where they were to proclaim their allegiance to the Lord as His people. There God renewed His covenant with the people and took it to another level by giving them the Law.

Although the Law was not the complete fulfillment of God's heart protection plan, it accomplished several important things. The Law revealed both the righteous, holy nature of God and the sinful, unrighteous nature of man. It set out God's standards and exposed man's utter inability to meet those standards. The Law provided a measure against which to judge the heart of man. Those who obeyed the Law, or sought to obey it, could be seen by God as having an obedient heart, whereas those who disobeyed, particularly in a habitual pattern, were shown to have a disobedient heart.

Saul, Israel's first king, was rejected by God because of his disobedience (see 1 Sam. 15). Saul's failure to obey the Lord revealed him to be a man with a disobedient heart. On the other hand, King David was a man of an obedient heart. He had many flaws and committed many sins, including adultery and murder, yet his heart was inclined to God. David loved the Lord and whenever he was confronted by his sins, he always repented sincerely and sought God's forgiveness. The obedient inclination of David's heart pleased God. In fact, God regarded David as "a man after His own heart" (1 Sam. 13:14).

The Law revealed much of what God is like and taught the people what He expected from His children. The daily sacrifice of a lamb reminded the people that the forgiveness of their sins required the death of a sinless innocent and pointed ahead to the day when the spotless Lamb of God would die and take away the sins of the world. It helped prepare the people's heart to receive their Messiah whenever He would be revealed. It called on them to love God with all their heart.

In fact, the Law served *primarily* as a teacher to prepare the way for the coming of Jesus. This is how the apostle Paul understood it. He wrote to the Galatians:

> But before faith came, we were kept under the law, shut up unto the faith which should afterwards be revealed. Wherefore **the law was our schoolmaster to bring us unto Christ**, that we might be justified by faith. But after that faith is come, we are no longer under a schoolmaster. For ye are all the children of God by faith in Christ Jesus (Galatians 3:23-26).

The Law also served as a form of *protection* for the people. Since the beginning, satan and God have been at war over the *heart* of men. The activity of satan is present in the Old Testament but is not clearly seen. With few exceptions, such as the Book of Job, satan works behind the scenes deceiving through false teachings; tempting through lust, sin, adultery, and fornication; and encouraging idolatry and rebellion. God gave the Law to show His people the right way to live, to expose the lies and deception of the enemy, and to set the Lord's people apart as a distinct nation holy and dedicated to Him.

As good as the Law was, the people failed to obey it and therefore came under God's judgment. The Law exposed sin for what it is and revealed God's righteous and holy standards, but it did not provide the *power* to live according to those standards. According to God's purpose, the Law was incomplete in itself. Only in Jesus Christ would it find complete fulfillment. The Law by itself was not God's ultimate plan; it was *preparation* for the coming of Christ. The power to live by God's standards would come only by receiving the new heart that He could give.

Protected by the Lamb

The death of Christ to wash away the sins of the world and to provide a new heart for men was in the heart of God from the beginning. Revelation 13:8 speaks of Jesus Christ as "the Lamb slain from the foundation of the world." In his first Letter the apostle Peter writes that we are not redeemed with corruptible things of the world, "But with the precious blood of Christ, as of a *lamb* without blemish and without spot: who verily *was foreordained before the foundation of the world*" (1 Pet. 1:19-20a). All throughout Old Testament times the coming of Christ was being prepared in the heart of God. Jesus came when the time was right, ushering in a new phase of God's plan. Paul understood this and explained it to the Galatians this way:

> *But when the fulness of the time was come, God sent*
> *forth His Son, made of a woman, made under the law,*
> *to redeem them that were under the law, that we might*
> *receive the adoption of sons* (Galatians 4:4-5).

Our condition was so desperate that the only hope was for God Himself to enter our heart and change us from the inside. This is why Christ was born. He came down through time and generations, entered Mary's womb, and was born into the world of man. The Son of God walked as the Son of man so that we might walk as sons of God. He became a man formed not just in God's likeness and image but identical to Him in every way. Jesus had neither the seed of sinful Adam nor the thought patterns and words of men; He had only those of God. Jesus thought as His Father thought, spoke what His Father spoke, and did what His Father did, showing forth in every way God's perfect will (see Jn. 5:17,19-20). His heart was God's heart. His mind was God's mind. His words were God's words. As Paul told the Colossians, Jesus was the full, perfect representation of God in the flesh:

> **Who is the image of the invisible God**, *the firstborn*
> *of every creature: for by Him were all things created,*
> *that are in heaven, and that are in earth, visible and*
> *invisible, whether they be thrones, or dominions, or*
> *principalities, or powers: all things were created by*
> *Him, and for Him: and He is before all things, and by*
> *Him all things consist....For* **in Him dwelleth all the**
> **fulness of the Godhead bodily** (Colossians 1:15-17;
> 2:9).

The Son of God came as a man before men in order to show forth the heart of God, that men may identify with Him heart-to-heart, may recognize the kind of heart they need, and may come to Him for a heart transplant (change). He came to give us a new heart so that we may have a way to enter into the heart of God. Jesus manifested the heart of God in the earth so that our heart may be as His heart and so that we, in turn, may manifest God's heart in the earth, may please God, and may be God-approved.

Jesus came into the world to provide us with the benefits of God's heart protection plan. We needed a covering to protect us and to deliver us from the works and effects of sin. Just as an umbrella covers us and protects us from the rain, so Jesus' blood covers us, protects us, and gives life and vigor to our new heart.

Of course, Jesus had to die in order for His blood to cover us. This was part of God's plan. Ordinarily a will cannot be probated until after the death of the testator. In the same way, God's heart protection plan could not go into full effect until after Jesus had died and had been raised to life again. The Book of Hebrews tells us:

> How much more shall the blood of **Christ**, who through the eternal Spirit offered Himself without spot to God, purge your conscience from dead works to serve the living God? And for this cause He **is the mediator of the new testament**, that by means of death, for the redemption of the transgressions that were under the first testament, they which are called might receive the promise of eternal inheritance. For **where a testament is, there must also of necessity be the death of the testator**. For a testament is of force after men are dead: otherwise **it is of no strength at all while the testator liveth** (Hebrews 9:14-17).

Jesus died to put into effect our spiritual heart protection plan. He didn't go to the cross just to die for our sins. He went to the cross so that we could live in God and inherit eternal life. When we receive Him in faith, He enters into us through the Holy Spirit, changes our heart, cleanses us from our sin, and makes us righteous and holy. We become children of God who have a heart like His and who come under His heart protection plan.

When you contract for an insurance policy and the premium has been paid, all that is necessary for it to be valid is for you to sign the policy. Then it is in effect. Jesus does the same for us in our heart. When we invite Him in through faith, He writes our name in the Lamb's Book of Life (see Rev. 13:8), in effect signing the protection plan for which He has already paid the premium. We are now protected, and the Holy Spirit seals our heart as belonging to God: "Now He which stablisheth us with you in Christ, and hath anointed us, is God; who hath also sealed us, and given the earnest of the Spirit in our hearts" (2 Cor. 1:21-22); "...after that ye believed, ye were sealed with that holy Spirit of promise, which is the earnest of our inheritance until the redemption of the purchased possession..." (Eph. 1:13-14).

Protected by the Spirit

Ephesians 4:30 says that through the Holy Spirit believers have been "sealed unto the day of redemption." This is another part of God's heart protection plan. He dwells in us through the Spirit so that He may protect our heart. He seals our heart against the arrows of lust, adultery, rebellion, lying, hatred, and all other deeds of wickness that satan fires at us. We are sealed as belonging to God. Our heart is protected and inclined toward God. This is why King David was able to say when he fell into sin:

Have mercy upon me, O God, according to Thy lovingkindness: according unto the multitude of Thy tender mercies blot out my transgressions. Wash me thoroughly from mine iniquity, and cleanse me from my sin....Create in me a clean heart, O God; and renew a right spirit within me. Cast me not away from Thy presence; and take not Thy holy spirit from me.

*Restore unto me the joy of Thy salvation; and uphold
me with Thy free spirit* (Psalm 51:1-2,10-12).

Because David's heart was inclined toward God, it was
sealed and protected, and David enjoyed God's favor and
forgiveness:

*Blessed is he whose transgression is forgiven, whose sin
is covered....I acknowledged my sin unto Thee, and
mine iniquity have I not hid. I said, I will confess my
transgressions unto the Lord; and Thou forgavest the
iniquity of my sin...* (Psalm 32:1,5).

The Holy Spirit not only seals us unto the day of redemption but also teaches us the ways of God. He leads us into the
knowledge of spiritual truth and reminds us of the things
Jesus taught. Jesus promised His disciples that "the Com-
forter, which is the Holy Ghost, whom the Father will send in
My name, He shall teach you all things, and bring all things to
your remembrance, whatsoever I have said unto you" (Jn.
14:26).

Unlike the Law, which could not enable the people to
obey, the Holy Spirit gives us the *power* to live in a manner
that pleases God and fulfills His will and purpose. As the
apostle Paul explained to the Romans:

*There is therefore now no condemnation to them
which are in Christ Jesus, who walk not after the flesh,
but after the Spirit. For* **the law of the Spirit of life in
Christ Jesus hath made me free from the law of sin
and death.** *For what the law could not do, in that it
was weak through the flesh, God sending His own Son
in the likeness of sinful flesh, and for sin, condemned
sin in the flesh: that* **the righteousness of the law
might be fulfilled in us, who walk not after the flesh,
but after the Spirit** (Romans 8:1-4).

Through the Spirit Jesus administers to us a *new covenant* that is superior to the old one and is written on our heart rather than on tablets of stone as was the Law (see Heb. 8:6-13; 12:24). The new heart that Jesus gives us is inclined toward God rather than toward sin because God's law, the "law of the Spirit of life in Christ Jesus" is written on it. In this way we become "the epistle of Christ...written not with ink, but with the Spirit of the living God; not in tables of stone, but in fleshly tables of the heart" (2 Cor. 3:3).

The protection we receive when we "give our heart" to Jesus is far greater than the protection that was available under the Law alone. Jesus *secured* our heart protection plan through His death and resurrection. The indwelling Holy Spirit *seals* the plan in our life.

God expects His children to have a clean, pure, and perfect heart. Jesus gives us a new heart that meets God's demands, but we also bear the responsibility for the condition of that heart. Even as Christians our heart can become dirty, rebellious, lustful, and deceitful. That's why it is important for us to undergo regular "heart examinations." We need to let the Spirit of God search our heart and show us its condition. A heart secured by Christ and sealed by the Spirit can be cleansed and renewed through confession and repentance.

The remaining chapters of this book will focus on a detailed "examination" of the things required in a heart that is right and pleasing before God: faith (belief and trust), purity, love, joy, peace, faithfulness, power, and victory.

Do you have God's heart protection plan in operation in your life? Is your heart clean and pure before Him? Make sure that you have given your heart to God *completely*. Most people haven't. That's why Jesus said that only a few will find the path that leads to life:

> *Enter ye in at the strait gate: for wide is the gate, and broad is the way, that leadeth to destruction, and many there be which go in thereat: because strait is the gate,*

and narrow is the way, which leadeth unto life, and few there be that find it (Matthew 7:13-14).

Salvation must be from the *heart*. Eternal life must dwell in the *heart*. Jesus stands ready to give a new heart to anyone who asks; He is ready to place anyone who comes to Him under God's heart protection plan. Don't miss out! Be one of those whose heart is under God's divine seal and protection. Be one of those who find the strait gate and the narrow way that lead to life!

Endnotes

1. James Strong, *Strong's Exhaustive Concordance of the Bible* (Peabody, MA: Hendrickson Publishers, n.d.) #H6754.
2. I want to make it clear at this point, if it is not already, that throughout this book the word *heart* refers to the inner man, the spiritual being that is the very core of who we are as individuals. If reference to the physical blood-pumping organ is intended, it either will be stated directly or will be clear from the context.
3. *Strong's*, #H1320 and #H1319.
4. R. Laird Harris, Gleason L. Archer, Jr. and Bruce K. Waltke, eds. *Theological Wordbook of the Old Testament* (Chicago: Moody Press, 1980), 1:135-136, **flesh** (#291a).
5. *Strong's*, #H7307.

Chapter 3

A Believing Heart

*But what saith it? The word is nigh thee, even in thy mouth, and in thy heart: that is, the word of faith, which we preach; that if thou shalt confess with thy mouth the Lord Jesus, and shalt **believe** in thine heart that God hath raised Him from the dead, thou shalt be saved. For with the heart man **believeth** unto righteousness; and with the mouth confession is made unto salvation (Romans 10:8-10).*

Faith is at the very *core* of a heart and life that are pleasing to God. Proverbs 4:23 says that from the heart flow the issues of life. Our life reflects what is in our heart. A life of faith flows from a believing heart and only a *believing heart* is pleasing to God. One example of such a pleasing life is that of Enoch. Genesis 5:24 says, "And Enoch walked with God: and he was not; for God took him." The word *walked* here means more than just a literal walk; it refers to a whole manner of life. Enoch lived a life of faith in continual fellowship with God and God "took him." The writer of Hebrews provides additional insight:

By faith Enoch was translated [taken away] *that he should not see death; and was not found, because God*

*had translated him: for before his translation **he had
this testimony, that he pleased God.** But **without
faith it is impossible to please Him:** for he that
cometh to God must believe that He is, and that He is
a rewarder of them that diligently seek Him* (Hebrews
11:5-6).

Enoch walked with God because he had a believing heart.
He pleased God, so he was spared death and taken straight
into God's presence. What a life of faith he must have had!

The critical importance of faith is made crystal clear in
verse 6: "without faith it is *impossible* to please Him [God]."
The Greek word for "impossible" is *adunatos*, which also
means "weak," "impotent," and "unable to do."[1] Without
faith we are powerless (impotent) to please God; that is, we
are completely unable to make ourselves acceptable to Him.

Obviously then, faith is the *starting place* for knowing and
pleasing God. God-pleasing faith *must* be *faith from the heart*.

The Heart of Faith

One of the clearest descriptions of faith is found in the
Book of Hebrews:

*Now faith is the substance of things hoped for, the evi-
dence of things not seen* (Hebrews 11:1).

The Greek word *pistis* (faith) can also be translated "belief"
or "assurance."[2] Its primary meaning is that of " 'firm persua-
sion,' a conviction based upon hearing...[and] is used in the
N[ew] T[estament] always of 'faith in God or Christ, or things
spiritual.' "[3] *Pistis* and its corresponding verb form *pisteuo*
(believe) have a much deeper meaning than simple mental
acceptance of facts. Biblical *pistis* involves "a firm conviction,
producing a full acknowledgment of God's revelation or
truth...a personal surrender to Him...[and] a conduct inspired
by such surrender."[4] In other words, God-pleasing faith is
active, not passive; it involves both *belief* and *behavior*. Our

behavior is determined by the condition of our heart. If we *believe* in our heart (if faith dwells in our inmost self), our *behavior* will reflect our faith.

A believing heart produces good works (behavior) as proof of faith. We read in the Book of James:

> *What doth it profit, my brethren,* **though a man say he hath faith, and have not works? can faith save him?** *If a brother or sister be naked, and destitute of daily food, and one of you say unto them, Depart in peace, be ye warmed and filled; notwithstanding ye give them not those things which are needful to the body; what doth it profit?* **Even so faith, if it hath not works, is dead,** *being alone* (James 2:14-17).

A few verses earlier, James gives a practical definition of faith from a believing heart:

> *Pure religion and undefiled before God and the Father is this, to visit the fatherless and widows in their affliction, and to keep himself unspotted from the world* (James 1:27).

According to God's Word, "faith" that is nothing more than words—no matter how good they sound—is not real faith. Right behavior and good works that honor God *reveal* that true faith is *already* lodged in our heart. Good works and right behavior never *produce* faith; they are the *results* of faith.

Hebrews 11:1 says that "faith is the *substance* of things *hoped for,* the *evidence* of things not seen." "Substance" in the Greek is *hupostasis,* which also means "assurance" and "confidence."[5] The word literally means " 'a standing under... that which stands, or is set, under, a foundation, beginning'; hence, the quality of confidence which leads one to stand under, endure, or undertake anything."[6] "Hoped for" is *elpizo,* which also means "to expect" or "trust,"[7] while "evidence" is translated from *elegchos,* which also means "proof" and "conviction."[8] Biblical, God-pleasing faith then is a confident expectancy that God will be true to His Word; a belief that does not depend on sight ("seeing is believing" is *not* biblical faith!); and a confidence so secure that we are willing to "stand under" it or stake our life on it. The New International Version translates the verse this way: "Now faith is *being sure of* what we hope for and *certain of* what we do not see." It is the kind of faith Paul had in mind when he wrote, "For we walk by faith, not by sight" (2 Cor. 5:7).

Faith Unto Salvation

The most important aspect for people of faith from the heart is that it be a faith that leads to salvation:

> *But what saith it?* **The word** *is nigh thee, even in thy mouth, and* **in thy heart**: *that is,* **the word of faith,** *which we preach; that* **if thou shalt** *confess with thy mouth the Lord Jesus, and shalt* **believe in thine heart** *that God hath raised Him from the dead,* **thou shalt be saved.** *For* **with the heart man believeth unto righteousness**; *and with the mouth confession is made* **unto salvation** (Romans 10:8-10).

There are two very important and closely related words in these verses: *saved* and *salvation*. The Greek word for "saved" is *sozo*; for "salvation" it is *soteria*. *Sozo* means "to deliver or protect," "to heal," "to preserve," and "to be (make) whole."[9] *Soteria*, which is derived from *soter*, a noun meaning "a deliverer,"[10] denotes "deliverance" and "preservation."[11] In this verse, *soteria* specifically refers to "the spiritual and eternal deliverance granted immediately by God to those who accept His conditions of repentance and faith in the Lord Jesus, in whom alone it is to be obtained...and upon confession of Him as Lord."[12]

"Righteousness" in the Greek is *dikaiosune*, which in this verse means to be "brought into right relationship with God."[13] The word also means "right action."[14] It is with our *heart* that we believe "unto righteousness." In other words, repentance and faith in Jesus from the heart make us right with God, and being right with God is part of what it means to be saved. Salvation (being saved) is the completed work of God on the hidden man of the heart.

The Greek word *homologeo* ("confess," "confession") literally means "to speak the same thing...to assent, accord, agree with."[15] As used in these verses, the word means "to declare openly by way of speaking out freely, such confession being the effect of deep conviction of facts."[16] To "confess... the Lord Jesus" means more than simply to say the words, "Jesus is Lord." Anyone can do that. True "confession" here means to openly acknowledge that Jesus is Lord from a deep *heartfelt belief* and conviction that it is true. Remember that faith from the heart involves both belief and behavior. What we *believe* in our inner self, our "hidden man of the heart," determines our outward *behavior*. If we truly *believe in our heart* that Jesus is Lord, then that belief will be reflected in what we do and say.

Saving faith is faith that depends on Jesus Christ's finished work on the cross as the *only* basis for the forgiveness of our sins, for our receiving the gift of eternal life, and for our entrance into Heaven. It is the total commitment of our life to following Christ in obedience to His Word.

*Our heart **condition** determines our eternal **position**.* If our heart is not right, we are not right, no matter what we say or do. This is the tragic state of every unbeliever. Unless their unbelieving heart is changed through faith into a believing heart and they are made right with God, they will never enjoy eternal life and see the Kingdom of Heaven.

I believe there is also a major problem in the Church today over this very point. How many church people do you know whose speech and outward behavior do not seem to "confess...the Lord Jesus"? If you are a Christian, before you get too judgmental, take a look at *yourself.* Do *your* actions clearly declare before men, "Jesus is Lord"? Does *your* speech leave no doubt that you *believe in your heart* that God raised Him from the dead? Is your heart right with God? Do your actions and lifestyle prove it?

Daily or weekly self-judgment of the heart is crucial as the days grow more evil. I believe that the Lord commends righteous judgment in which we are to judge ourselves. If we don't judge ourselves (our heart), we will be judged of God.

As God has spoken to me during my ministry over the years, I have come to the realization through experience and observation that *many church people have mouth confession without heart possession.* God-pleasing faith has never become implanted in their heart. I know that I can't tell for sure where anyone else stands with God, but I have seen a lot of church people whose life shows no outward evidence of an inward heart change. I do believe, sadly, that there are many lost people who are walking around in our churches masquerading as believers and confessing yet sinning.

Another difficulty in the Church is the number of genuine believers who have a spiritual heart problem. In this case it is a matter of *too much mouth confession with too little heart possession.* Where salvation is concerned, we either possess saving faith or we do *not* possess saving faith. We either have it or we don't. Although we may possess saving faith, the question is, does it possess *us?* We believe and confess Jesus as Lord, but our heart is not pure and clean before God because we have not surrendered ourselves completely to Him. We feel guilty, weak, defeated, and fearful, with no joy, peace, or victory. Christians! It's time for us to wake up and tend to our heart! We lack victory in our life and power in our churches because our heart is not right before God! We need to come to God in humility and repentance, surrender our heart to Him, and ask Him to make it right before Him. There's no time to lose! The Church's heart condition is *critical!*

Principles of Faith

In his Gospel, Matthew records a dialogue between Jesus and His disciples that is important for our understanding of faith from the heart:

> When Jesus came into the coasts of Caesarea Philippi, He asked His disciples, saying, Whom do men say that I the Son of man am? And they said, Some say that Thou art John the Baptist: some, Elias; and others, Jeremias, or one of the prophets. He saith unto them, But whom say ye that I am? And Simon Peter answered and said, Thou art the Christ, the Son of the living God. And Jesus answered and said unto him, Blessed art thou, Simon Barjona: for flesh and blood hath not revealed it unto thee, but My Father which is in heaven (Matthew 16:13-17).

This exchange reveals several significant principles of faith:

1. *Faith centers around knowing **who** Jesus is.* With His pointed question, "Whom say ye that I am?" Jesus was trying to gauge the disciples' faith (heart) condition. (And trying to help them recognize it for themselves!) The disciples knew what *others* were saying (v. 14); now Jesus wanted to know what they believed. He wanted them to know who He was.

2. *Faith is in a **Person**, not a doctrine.* Peter's declaration, "Thou art the Christ, the Son of the living God," was an expression of faith in the *person* of Jesus. Peter's faith was not in the teachings of Jesus or even in any of His miracles; rather, Peter's faith was in Jesus as a Person, the Son of God. Faith from the heart has *always* been faith in the Person of God. In Genesis we read of Abraham that "he *believed in the Lord*; and He [the Lord] counted it to him [Abraham] for righteousness" (Gen. 15:6). The Gospel of John says, "For God so loved the world, that He gave His only begotten Son, that

whosoever believeth in Him should not perish, but have ever-lasting life" (Jn. 3:16).

3. *Faith is a gift from God.* After commending Peter for his faith, Jesus told him, "flesh and blood hath not revealed it unto thee, but My Father which is in heaven." Peter's faith to believe in Jesus was given to him by God the Father. In his Letter to the Ephesians Paul makes this statement: "For by grace are ye saved through faith; and that not of yourselves: *it is the gift of God*: not of works, lest any man should boast" (Eph. 2:8-9). The basis of salvation is grace *and* faith acting together in our heart to produce repentance. God's grace, which saves us, and the faith by which we receive it are both indispensable parts of salvation, the whole of which is the gift of God. He gives us the grace; He also gives us the faith to believe.

4. *Faith is personal.* Although Peter may have been speaking for the band of disciples as a whole when he made his statement of faith, Jesus' words were directed at Peter personally: "Blessed art thou, Simon Barjona..." (Mt. 16:16). In addition to Peter's personal name, the phrase "art thou" in the Greek is in the second person singular form.[17] God revealed this faith to Peter *personally* and *individually*. Faith is uniquely personal. Faith is "you-designed" and "me-designed." You cannot live on or by anyone else's faith, and neither can I. We each must have our own. The old saying is true: "God has no grandchildren."

Walking by Faith

This kind of faith—*personal* faith in the *Person* of Jesus Christ as the Son of God and as Lord and Savior—settles our heart, mind, and spirit in God. It focuses our attention on Him rather than on ourselves. This faith from the heart leads us to recognize that God's point of view on things is much more important than our own. Before any of us can make sense out of life or experience much growth as Christians, we must learn to see life from God's point of view. This means basing our decisions and actions on what God says even if His word goes against the so-called "wisdom" or "knowledge" of the world.

Sometimes doing what God says won't make sense by the world's standards. This really should not surprise us since God tells us in His Word: "My thoughts are not your thoughts, neither are your ways My ways....For as the heavens are higher than the earth, so are My ways higher than your ways, and My thoughts than your thoughts" (Is. 55:8-9). Furthermore, Scripture teaches us that the world cannot understand the things or the ways of God: "But the natural man [the world] receiveth not the things of the Spirit of God: for they are foolishness unto him: neither can he know them, because they are spiritually discerned" (1 Cor. 2:14).

Following God rather than the world is what the apostle Paul was referring to when he wrote, "For we walk by faith, not by sight" (2 Cor. 5:7). The world as a whole lives by the philosophy that "seeing is believing." Walking by faith rather than by sight does not mean "blind faith," but faith illuminated and informed by the promises and indwelling presence of the Person of Jesus Christ through the Holy Spirit. To walk by faith is to walk in the Spirit. It is a daily *spiritual* journey that denies the ungodly things of the world. As Paul wrote to the Galatians, "This I say then, Walk in the Spirit, and ye shall not fulfil the lust of the flesh....If we live in the Spirit, let us also walk in the Spirit" (Gal. 5:16,25).

Walking by faith from the heart is a lifestyle of trusting and obeying God. Obedience involves faithfulness and is motivated by love. If we love God we will obey Him, and obeying Him means being faithful to Him. It means standing ready to do whatever He asks of us. Jesus said to His disciples, "If ye love Me, keep My commandments" (Jn. 14:15). If we love the Lord we will be faithful to Him in our words, our thoughts, and our actions. In our human relationships we want to do things for those we love that will please them and bring them joy. We do it out of our love for them. The same should be true of our relationship with God. If we are operating out of faith from the heart we will have the desire to please God because we love Him. The presence and power of the Holy Spirit in us will enable us to be faithful. As our love grows, our faithfulness will grow as well.

We have a wonderful model and example for our faithfulness: the faithfulness of God Himself. God has always been faithful. It is His nature. Moses reminded the Israelites of this when he said, "Know therefore that the Lord thy God, He is God, *the faithful God*, which keepeth covenant and mercy with them that love Him and keep His commandments to a thousand generations" (Deut. 7:9). God is faithful "to a thousand generations" to those who love and obey Him. He renews His love and faithfulness every day: "It is of the Lord's mercies that we are not consumed, because *His compassions fail not. They are new every morning: great is Thy faithfulness*" (Lam. 3:22-23).

Walking by faith carries many benefits. A lifestyle of faithfulness to God brings to us a deep and growing assurance of our security in God. The Spirit of God gives us assurance in at least three areas:

1. *Our sins are forgiven.* Faith from the heart assures us that our sins have been forgiven in Christ. Paul wrote to the Ephesians, "Blessed be the God and Father of our Lord Jesus Christ, who hath blessed us with all spiritual blessings in heavenly places in Christ....*In whom we have* redemption through His blood, *the forgiveness of sins*, according to the riches of His grace" (Eph. 1:3,7). In his first Letter, John had this to say to some of his readers: "I write unto you, little children, because *your sins are forgiven you* for His name's sake" (1 Jn. 2:12). There is no feeling quite like the joy that comes when we know that our sins have been forgiven! David the psalmist expressed it so well when he wrote:

Blessed is he whose transgression is forgiven, whose sin is covered. Blessed is the man unto whom the Lord imputeth not iniquity, and in whose spirit there is no guile....I acknowledged my sin unto Thee, and mine iniquity have I not hid. I said, I will confess my transgressions unto the Lord; and Thou forgavest the iniquity of my sin... (Psalm 32:1-2,5).

2. *We can overcome temptation.* Faith from the heart gives us the power to overcome temptation—a power we did not have before we were saved. That power comes from the Holy Spirit, who lives in us and is a reflection of God's faithfulness: "There hath no temptation taken you but such as is common to man: but *God is faithful*, who will not suffer you to be tempted above that ye are able; but *will with the temptation also make a way to escape, that ye may be able to bear it*" (1 Cor. 10:13). This power to overcome temptation is realized by those who have a *believing heart*—those who trust in God, relying on His strength rather than on human effort. Overcoming temptation in the power of the Spirit also leads to great blessing: "*Blessed is the man that endureth temptation*: for when he is tried, *he shall receive the crown of life*, which the Lord hath promised to them that love Him" (Jas. 1:12).

3. *We have full assurance of our salvation.* Faith from the heart helps us know for sure that we are saved. Do you have that assurance? Do you know *in your heart* that you are saved, secure in God's grace? Such assurance comes through the Holy Spirit: "The Spirit Himself bears witness with our spirit that we are children of God, and if children, then heirs; heirs of God and joint heirs with Christ" (Rom. 8:16-17a NKJ). God doesn't want any of His children to be in doubt over his or her eternal position. He wants us to *know* with *absolute confidence*, as we walk by faith, that we are His children. John makes this perfectly clear toward the end of his first Letter when he writes:

*And this is the record, that **God hath given to us eternal life, and this life is in His Son. He that hath the Son hath life**; and he that hath not the Son of God hath not life. **These things have I written** unto you that believe on the name of the Son of God; **that ye may know that ye have eternal life**, and that ye may believe on the name of the Son of God* (1 John 5:11-13).

Steps to a Believing Heart

So where do *you* stand? What's the condition of your heart? Are you walking in faith from a living, believing heart made clean and new through the blood of Christ? Have you ever experienced the joy of having your sins forgiven and your heart made right with God? Either you are a member of the Kingdom of God or you are not. Either you have a believing heart or you do not. There is no middle ground.

There's no better time than right now to settle the matter between you and God. The steps to a believing heart are easy:

1. *Realize that God loves you and wants the very best for you.*

For God so loved the world, that He gave His only begotten Son, that whosoever believeth in Him should not perish, but have everlasting life (John 3:16).

For I know the thoughts that I think toward you, says the Lord, thoughts of peace and not of evil, to give you a future and a hope. Then you will call upon Me and go and pray to Me, and I will listen to you. And you will seek Me and find Me, when you search for Me with all your heart (Jeremiah 29:11-13 NKJ).

2. *Recognize that you are a sinner in need of God's grace and forgiveness.*

They are all gone aside, they are all together become filthy: there is none that doeth good, no, not one (Psalm 14:3).

For all have sinned, and come short of the glory of God (Romans 3:23).

3. *Acknowledge that your sins have separated you from God.*

But your iniquities have separated between you and your God, and your sins have hid His face from you, that He will not hear (Isaiah 59:2).

For the wages of sin is death [eternal separation from God] (Romans 6:23a).

4. *Believe that Jesus Christ, the Son of God, died for your sins so that you might have eternal life.*

...but the gift of God is eternal life through Jesus Christ our Lord (Romans 6:23).

Therefore being justified by faith, we have peace with God through our Lord Jesus Christ....For when we were yet without strength, in due time Christ died for the ungodly....But God commendeth His love toward us, in that, while we were yet sinners, Christ died for us (Romans 5:1,6,8).

For God so loved the world, that He gave His only begotten Son, that whosoever believeth in Him should not perish, but have everlasting life (John 3:16).

5. *Confess your faith in Jesus for the forgiveness of your sins and give Him control of your heart and life as Lord and Savior.*

If we confess our sins, He is faithful and just to forgive us our sins, and to cleanse us from all unrighteousness (1 John 1:9).

That if thou shalt confess with thy mouth the Lord Jesus, and shalt believe in thine heart that God hath raised Him from the dead, thou shalt be saved....For whosoever shall call upon the name of the Lord shall be saved (Romans 10:9,13).

Maybe you already know Jesus as your Savior and Lord. That's great. Even so, your heart may not be right before Him. Each of us can benefit from a periodic heart examination. Christian brother or sister, go to the Lord in prayer and ask Him to show you the condition of your heart and to set right whatever may be out of place. You may want to pray according to the closing words of Psalm 139: "Search me, O God, and *know my heart*: try me, and *know my thoughts*: and see if there be any wicked way in me, and *lead me in the way everlasting*" (Ps. 139:23-24).

Endnotes

1. James Strong, *Strong's Exhaustive Concordance of the Bible* (Peabody, MA: Hendrickson Publishers, n.d.), #G102.
2. *Strong's*, #G4102.
3. W.E. Vine, Merrill F. Unger, and William White, Jr. *Vine's Complete Expository Dictionary of Old and New Testament Words* (Nashville: Thomas Nelson Publishers, 1985), p. 222.
4. *Vine's*, p. 222.
5. *Strong's*, #G5287.
6. *Vine's*, pp. 120-121.
7. *Strong's*, #G1679.
8. *Strong's*, #G1650.
9. *Strong's*, #G4982.
10. *Strong's*, *soter*, #G4990.
11. *Vine's*, p. 545.
12. *Vine's*, p. 545.
13. *Vine's*, p. 535.
14. *Vine's*, p. 535.
15. *Vine's*, p. 120.
16. *Vine's*, p. 120.
17. *Strong's*, #G1488.

Chapter 4

A Pure Heart

Blessed are the pure in heart: for they shall see God (Matthew 5:8).

I've always loved milk. For me there's almost nothing better than the taste of cold milk—so cold that it is almost ice. Most of you, I'm sure, remember the humorous milk commercials on television that show people in various situations getting frantic when they find themselves without milk at a time when they really want it. The ad's simple slogan was, "Got milk?"® That's me. I could've been one of the people in those ads.

One day when I was really thirsty I poured for myself a tall glass of milk. I was practically licking my lips in anticipation of its cool refreshing. Before I could take my first sip, however, a fly rose to the top of the glass. Instantly my attitude changed. My anticipation evaporated. The milk that had been so inviting a moment before was suddenly repugnant to me. I couldn't trust it. I wouldn't drink it. I didn't want to put it into my body. Instead, I poured it down the drain; in fact, I dumped not just the glass, but the entire gallon it had come from! The milk had completely lost its appeal. It had looked fine on the outside; judging from the container and the milk's color and smell, it appeared to be normal. There was something wrong *inside*, however. As far as I was concerned, the milk was *unclean* and unacceptable.

Like my tainted milk, most of us wouldn't dream of eating spoiled food, drinking contaminated water, or otherwise deliberately taking into our body anything we consider to be unclean or harmful (although many people smoke and/or drink or take drugs while fully aware of the health risks— these often involve addiction, which is different). We keep our body clean and tend to be very careful about how we present ourselves to other people. We give a lot of attention to external cleanliness and to preventing uncleanness from getting inside. Unfortunately, *we often ignore the uncleanness that is already inside us—the impurity of our heart.*

Whited Sepulchres

During one of His frequent run-ins with the scribes and Pharisees, Jesus had some blunt, harsh words for them:

> *Woe unto you, scribes and Pharisees, hypocrites! for ye make* **clean** *the* **outside** *of the cup and of the platter,* **but within** *they are* **full of extortion and excess**. *Thou blind Pharisee,* **cleanse first that which is within** *the cup and platter,* **that the outside** *of them* **may be clean also**. *Woe unto you, scribes and Pharisees, hypocrites!* **for ye are like unto whited sepulchres, which indeed appear beautiful outward, but are within full of dead men's bones, and of all uncleanness**. *Even so ye also* **outwardly appear righteous** *unto men, but* **within ye are full of hypocrisy and iniquity** (Matthew 23:25-28).

By all outward appearances these scribes and Pharisees were without fault. Highly respected for their knowledge of the Law and widely popular because of their unwavering allegiance to it, these men were the pillars of Jewish society. They enjoyed the best seats in the synagogues and the places of highest honor at banquets and celebrations. Jesus, however, who knows the heart of all men, saw them for who they really were—hypocrites who had put on a "religious" whitewash to cover up the spiritual uncleanness and impurity of their heart. Outward religious piety masked inward ungodliness.

The scribes and Pharisees probably found particularly offensive Jesus' comparison of them to "whited sepulchres... full of dead men's bones and...uncleanness." According to the Law these men revered so highly, anything dead was unclean and anyone who came into the slightest contact with anything dead became unclean. These Jewish religious leaders were very scrupulous in avoiding even the tiniest violation of the Law (or so they thought). I'm sure that being compared to perpetually unclean tombs did not sit well with them!

When other people looked at these leaders, they saw righteousness and respectability. When Jesus looked at them, He saw extortion ("pillage, plundering, robbery"),[1] excess ("self-indulgence"),[2] uncleanness ("impurity"),[3] hypocrisy ("acting under a feigned part, deceit"),[4] and iniquity ("illegality, violation of law").[5]

Jesus criticized the scribes and Pharisees because they acted religious and righteous while their heart was unclean and impure before God. I believe this has become a very real problem in the Church today also. Make no mistake about it, our churches are full of uncleanness: impure thoughts, lust, fornication, adultery, greed, hatred, bitterness, rebellion, disobedience—you name it. Impure hearts hinder our love for God and our commitment to Christ. They rob us of our joy, our power, our praise and worship, and our effectiveness in ministry. They deceive us into thinking that we're right with God when actually, or in reality, we are very far away from Him. We need to regard Jesus' words to the scribes and Pharisees as a warning also for *us* to take a close look at the purity of our own heart.

When we examine our heart we need to remember that things are not always as they seem to be. We need to learn to see ourselves not as we think we are or as others see us, but as God sees us. His point of view is different from ours.

Looks Can Be Deceiving

We live in a very shallow, superficial world. Virtually every aspect of our society discourages us from pressing below the surface to the real meanings that lie underneath. We have surface relationships, superficial conversations, and shallow concepts of truth and beauty; we pursue meaningless goals and make hollow promises. Rarely do we go below the surface, perhaps from fear of what we will find. None of us can probe very deep into ourselves without discovering things that we don't like. It's easier not to try.

We make decisions and judgments based on outward appearances, and years later are still suffering the consequences: bad marriages, domestic violence, rape, unwanted pregnancies, abortions, adultery, and the like. I'm not talking about just the lost world. *These things are happening in the Church too.* Many people, including Christians, suffer from depression, demonic oppression, low self-esteem, guilt, and self-condemnation. As James says, "My brethren, these things ought not to be so" (Jas. 3:10b NKJ). God does not condemn us; He frees us. It says in Romans, "There is therefore now no condemnation to them which are in Christ Jesus.... For *the law of the Spirit of life in Christ Jesus hath made me free* from the law of sin and death" (Rom. 8:1-2).

As Christians we must not look on outward appearance alone because looks can be deceiving. More importantly, we must not do so because God doesn't. He looks beyond the surface and probes right into the heart:

> *But the Lord said unto Samuel, Look not on his countenance, or on the height of his stature; because I have refused him: for the Lord seeth not as man seeth; for*

man looketh on the outward appearance, but the Lord looketh on the heart (1 Samuel 16:7).

Samuel, following God's instructions, had gone to Bethlehem to the house of Jesse in order to anoint one of Jesse's sons as the new king of Israel. The first king, Saul, had been a disappointment and God had purposed to remove the kingdom from him. Despite the fact that he was tall, strong, and good-looking—"kingly" in the opinion of the people—King Saul had failed because his *heart* was not clean and pure before God. Saul exhibited a pattern of disobedience toward God and a disregard for God's will. He had directly disobeyed God's command to thoroughly destroy the Amalekites, a *perennial* enemy of Israel. Instead, Saul had spared the Amalekite king and taken much plunder, prompting Samuel to pronounce God's judgment on him: "For rebellion is as the sin of witchcraft, and stubbornness is as iniquity and idolatry. *Because thou hast rejected the word of the Lord, He hath also rejected thee from being king*" (1 Sam. 15:23). A short time before this, Samuel had warned Saul that his pattern of disobedience would cost him his kingdom:

> But now **thy kingdom shall not continue:** *the Lord hath sought Him a man after His own heart, and the Lord hath commanded him to be captain over His people,* **because thou hast not kept that which the Lord commanded thee** (1 Samuel 13:14).

This verse also reveals the kind of person God was looking for: "the Lord hath sought Him a man *after His own heart.*" God wanted a king who would seek His will and reflect His heart. The Lord had found such a man among Jesse's sons.

One by one the sons of Jesse were brought before Samuel, but the Lord rejected them all. Finally, only Jesse's youngest son, David, was left. As David was presented to Samuel, God said to Samuel, "Arise, anoint him: for this is he" (1 Sam. 16:12b). David proved to be the greatest king Israel ever had.

Despite his human flaws that periodically led him into sin, David sought God's heart and loved God with all *his* heart. Because his heart was *clean* and *pure* before the Lord, David was able to write in Psalm 24:

> *Who shall ascend into the hill of the Lord? or who shall stand in His holy place?* **He that hath clean hands, and a pure heart***; who hath not lifted up his soul unto vanity, nor sworn deceitfully. He* **shall receive the blessing from the Lord, and righteousness from the God of his salvation** (Psalm 24:3-5).

When God looks beneath the surface of our life He expects to find clean hands and a pure heart—holy living that reflects a heart of righteousness.

Touch Not the Unclean Thing

One function of the Jewish Law was to teach the people about holiness and what it meant to be a holy nation under God. There were strict guidelines regarding what things were clean and unclean as well as specific procedures and rituals through which those who were unclean could become clean again. No one, not even the high priest, could enter the presence of God without going through ritual cleansing. To do otherwise—to profane the holy things of God—meant death. Every item used in the tabernacle and temple worship was cleansed and made holy by sprinkling the blood of an innocent sacrifice on it. This set these things apart exclusively for God's service. Even the priests were set apart in this way. God wanted His people to understand how utterly separate He was from anything corrupt, unclean, sinful, or evil—and that He wanted them to be the same way.

God has not changed. He still wants all His children to be pure and holy before Him. In his first Letter the apostle Peter wrote, "But as He which hath called you is holy, *so be ye holy in all manner of conversation*; because it is written, *Be ye holy; for I am holy"* (1 Pet. 1:15-16). Paul stressed the same truth in a letter to a church that was having problems with the whole idea of holy living:

> *Be ye not unequally yoked together with unbelievers: for what fellowship hath righteousness with unrighteousness? and what communion hath light with darkness? And what concord hath Christ with Belial? or what part hath he that believeth with an infidel? And what agreement hath the temple of God with idols? for* **ye are the temple of the living God**; *as God hath said, I will dwell in them, and walk in them; and I will be their God, and they shall be My people. Wherefore come out from among them, and* **be ye separate**, *saith the Lord, and* **touch not the unclean thing**; *and I will receive you, and will be a Father unto you, and ye shall be My sons and daughters, saith the Lord Almighty* (2 Corinthians 6:14-18).

Paul's point is that anything unholy or impure—whether a thought, word, action, relationship, habit, entertainment, or anything else—is completely incompatible and out of place with the holy ones of God.

The Church is the temple of the living God. We are supposed to be holy, free of all impure things. We are not to "touch" or have anything to do with any "unclean thing." The very day we each gave our heart to Christ we became clay in His hands. Then He, as the divine potter, began to reshape and remold us into holy vessels fit for His use. The tragedy is that there are a whole lot of unclean vessels in the Church. Our churches are full of people with an impure heart: pastors, deacons, and teachers; men, women, and children. It is a problem that afflicts, or has afflicted, all of us at one time or another. We need to ask ourselves, as in the proverb, "Who can say, I have made my heart clean, I am pure from my sin?" (Prov. 20:9) A careful, searching self-examination of the heart is appropriate for every one of us.

Just because we have accepted Jesus Christ as our personal Savior doesn't necessarily mean that our hearts are pure. We can still suffer from gospel strokes and spiritual heart attacks. Even though we're saved, our hearts may still harbor pride, bitterness, anger, unforgiveness, unbelief, envy, and lust. If we are not communicating with the Father on a personal level, if we have not surrendered our wills to Him completely, if His abundant life is not in evidence in our life, then we may also be suffering a hardening of the spiritual arteries. Like the five foolish virgins in Matthew 25:1-13, we could be in the right place yet still miss out on God's divine plan for our life. On Sunday morning many are in the right place but have the wrong heart. We cannot effectively serve a right God having a wrong heart.

Many believers claim to know and love Jesus Christ yet still are bound by drugs, alcohol, gambling, immoral sex, profanity, dishonesty, or worse. Week after week they suffer spiritual heart failure right in their church pew while their pastor pounds empty words onto their cold, dead chest.

The problem is that even though the Lord gives us a new spiritual heart when we are saved, we continue to allow ourselves to be controlled by our old, dirty, corrupt, irredeemable, sinful, lustful heart of flesh. Jesus said that we are known by the fruit we bear, and that good trees produce good fruit, and bad trees produce rotten fruit (see Mt. 12:33). Paul listed some of the rotten fruit of the flesh in his Letter to the Galatians:

> *Now the works of the flesh are evident, which are: adultery, fornication, uncleanness, lewdness, idolatry, sorcery, hatred, contentions, jealousies, outbursts of wrath, selfish ambitions, dissensions, heresies, envy, murders, drunkenness, revelries, and the like; of which I tell you beforehand, just as I also told you in time past, that those who practice such things will not inherit the kingdom of God* (Galatians 5:19-21 NKJ).

Whether or not we want to admit it, many of these same things fester in our own heart and infect our churches. Failing to obey the Lord, we "touch" unclean things—things of the world—whether in our mind or with our body. We think impure thoughts; harbor lust in our heart; put other people or things ahead of God in our life; and give place to anger, division, and evil thoughts toward others. We indulge our own selfish desires and ambitions, giving little place to holiness or to God's claim on our life. Gratifying the flesh, we grieve the Holy Spirit. No wonder we live in fear and defeat and with little evidence of God's power and presence in our life and in our churches! A holy God cannot dwell in an unclean temple, and an unholy heart cannot dwell in God's presence.

Clean Hands and a Pure Heart

What does it mean to have clean hands and a pure heart? Remember that our behavior reveals the true condition of our heart. In Psalm 24:4 David said that the ones who will stand in the presence of the Lord will be those with "clean hands, and a pure heart." The Hebrew word translated "clean" is *naqi*, which means "blameless," "innocent," or "guiltless"[6] and in this verse specifically refers to "innocent behavior and "ethical purity."[7] "Pure" translates the Hebrew word *bar*, which also means "choice," "clean," and "clear"[8] and comes from a root (*barar*) that means "purge, purify, choose, cleanse or make bright, test, or prove."[9] Having clean hands, therefore, means living and behaving in a blameless, upright manner; and a pure heart is a heart purged or cleansed of sin and evil and made bright or morally spotless. In a manner similar to the way gold or other precious metals are assayed (tested) for purity, a pure heart has been tested and proven by God.

Just how important is it really to have a pure heart? Jesus made it pretty clear in the Sermon on the Mount when He said, "Blessed are the *pure in heart*: for they *shall see God*" (Mt. 5:8). Here the word *pure* renders the Greek word *katharos*, which literally means "free from impure admixture, without blemish, spotless."[10] In this verse *katharos* carries the sense of ethical purity, as in being "free from corrupt desire."[11] The pure in heart shall "see God." *Optanomai* ("see") is a Greek word that means to see in the sense of "to gaze...with wide-open eyes, as at something remarkable."[12] It is closely related to another word, *horao*, which means "to discern clearly," "to experience," "to behold," "to perceive."[13] The pure in heart—those whose heart God has tested, proven, and found to be spotless and without blemish—will see God. They will gaze in wide-eyed amazement as they behold Him and experience His presence.

The same Greek word, *optanomai*, is found in Hebrews 12:14, "Follow peace with all men, and holiness, without which no man shall see the Lord." This verse states the same truth in a negative way. Another way to refer to purity of heart is to speak of holiness. The pure in heart live a holy life before God. Without holiness, no one will see God! Purity of heart, then, is pretty important! It's the difference between seeing God and not seeing God, between being in His presence and not being in His presence, between being saved or being lost!

From First Peter 1:15-16 we know that God requires us to be holy just as He is holy. How are we to do this? It is not possible within our own wisdom or strength. We cannot be holy or live holy in our flesh. The power to do what God requires lies beyond us. However, all things are possible with God (see Mt. 19:26). What God requires of us, He Himself also enables us to do. He has made it possible for us to walk in the Spirit and not fulfill the lusts of the flesh. Left to ourselves, we will manifest in our life the works of the flesh that Paul listed in Galatians 5:19-21. The Lord, on the other hand, wants to develop in us divine attributes—the spiritual fruit of "love, joy, peace, longsuffering, kindness, goodness, faithfulness, gentleness [and] self-control" (Gal. 5:22-23 NKJ)—so that we can live according to His riches in glory and be a light in the world to those who walk in darkness.

Cleaning Up Our Hearts

Jesus said that the things that defile a man come from within, from his heart:

> But *those things which* proceed out of the mouth **come forth from the heart**; and they **defile the man**. *For out of the heart proceed evil thoughts, murders, adulteries, fornications, thefts, false witness, blasphemies: These are the things which defile a man* (Matthew 15:18-20a).

How do we deal with the uncleanness in our heart? What do we do about the unholy thoughts and desires that fill our mind? How can we bring our sinful behavior under control and present ourselves to God as clean, holy temples?

1. *Humble yourself before God.* The Book of James tells us, "Draw nigh to God, and He will draw nigh to you. *Cleanse your hands*, ye sinners; and *purify your hearts*, ye double minded....*Humble yourselves* in the sight of the Lord, and He shall lift you up" (Jas. 4:8,10). Clean hands, a pure heart, and a humble spirit go together. None can exist without the others. It is only through humility that we can be clean and can enjoy the presence of God. The prophet Isaiah wrote, "For *thus saith the high and lofty One* that inhabiteth eternity, *whose name is Holy; I dwell* in the high and holy place, *with him also that is of a contrite and humble spirit*, to revive the spirit of the humble, and to revive the heart of the contrite ones" (Is. 57:15). We must come humbly before God, acknowledging our need to be cleansed.

2. *Confess your need for cleansing and repent from the heart before God.* The Lord stands ready, even eager, to forgive, cleanse, and restore us. John the apostle wrote, "*If we confess our sins, He is faithful and just to forgive us our sins, and to cleanse us* from all unrighteousness" (1 Jn. 1:9). Furthermore, it is written in the Book of Joel, "So *rend your heart*, and not your garments; *return to the Lord your God*,

for *He is gracious and merciful*, slow to anger, and of great kindness; and He relents from doing harm" (Joel 2:13 NKJ). To confess means to agree with God about what He has revealed to us of the condition of our heart. To repent means to make a deliberate decision of the will to turn from our sinful, selfish ways and follow God's way with our whole heart. Therefore, repentance is important not only before water baptism but throughout our life in Christ. Repentance before water baptism *prepares* the heart, and repentance afterward baptism *preserves* the heart. As we confess our sins or needs, we resist the temptation to become too proud to repent.

3. *Ask God to cleanse your heart, renew your mind, and restore your spirit.* King David expressed it well when he asked the Lord, *"Create in me a clean heart, O God; and renew a right spirit within me. Cast me not away from Thy presence; and take not Thy holy spirit from me"* (Ps. 51:10-11). Only God can purify our heart and mind, and it is only through His power that we can keep them pure. First Corinthians 2:16 says that, as Christians, we have the *mind of Christ*. Therefore, we should "be not conformed to this world: but be...transformed by the renewing of [our] mind, that [we] may prove what is that good, and acceptable, and perfect, will of God" (Rom. 12:2). God wants us to have a pure heart. He has commanded us to be holy. When we come to Him in humility and repentance, He will cleanse us in accordance with His will. A clean heart is a protected heart.

4. *Practice the daily presence of God through the Word and the Spirit.* God has given us His Word, the Bible, through which He speaks to us and teaches us. He also has given us His Spirit, through whom He dwells in us and enlightens us. There are no better heart cleansers and mind regulators than these. Consider these verses from the Psalms:

Thy word have I hid in mine heart, that I might not sin against Thee (Psalm 119:11).

Thy word is a lamp unto my feet, and a light unto my path (Psalm 119:105).

Blessed is the man *that walketh not in the counsel of the ungodly, nor standeth in the way of sinners, nor sitteth in the seat of the scornful. But* **his delight is in the law of the Lord; and in His law doth he meditate day and night**. *And he shall be like a tree planted by the rivers of water, that bringeth forth his fruit in his season; his leaf also shall not wither; and* **whatsoever he doeth shall prosper** (Psalm 1:1-3).

God gave us the Holy Spirit in order to make us like Christ. In fact, the word *Christian* means "little Christ." We are to be like Him in heart, mind, spirit, and will. The Holy Spirit in us brings that about. He transforms our heart, our mind, and our character to be like those of Jesus. As Paul wrote to the Romans:

And we know that all things work together for good to **those who love God**, *to those who are the called according to His purpose. For whom He foreknew,* **He also predestined to be conformed to the image of His Son**, *that He might be the firstborn among many brethren* (Romans 8:28-29 NKJ).

It is only the pure in heart who will see God; only those with clean hands will ascend the hill of the Lord and stand in His holy place. Let us daily use God's heart cleansers—which are faith, love, God's Word, and the Holy Spirit in action for our spiritual heart protection. Most assuredly, a dirty, filthy heart can never produce a pure and clean life that is pleasing to God. It is only through the cleansing of our heart and mind that we can receive the fullest blessings of God and experience the fullness of His presence and power in and through us. Let us come humbly before our God, confess the uncleanness of our heart and mind, and ask Him to forgive us, cleanse us, and renew us so that we can be conformed to the image of His

Son. Perhaps we should heed the wise words of Paul to his spiritual son Timothy:

> *Therefore if anyone cleanses himself from the latter* [works of dishonor], *he will be a vessel for honor, sanctified and useful for the Master, prepared for every good work. Flee also youthful lusts; but* **pursue righteousness, faith, love, peace** *with those who call on the Lord* **out of a pure heart** (2 Timothy 2:21-22 NKJ).

Endnotes

1. W.E. Vine, Merrill F. Unger, and William White, Jr. *Vine's Complete Expository Dictionary of Old and New Testament Words* (Nashville: Thomas Nelson Publishers, 1985), p. 219.
2. James Strong, *Strong's Exhaustive Concordance of the Bible* (Peabody, MA: Hendrickson Publishers, n.d.), *akrasia*, #G192.
3. *Strong's, akatharsia,* #G167.
4. *Strong's, hupokrisis,* #G5272
5. *Strong's, anomia,* #G458.
6. *Strong's,* #G5355.
7. R. Laird Harris, Gleason L. Archer, Jr., and Bruce K. Waltke, eds. *Theological Wordbook of the Old Testament* (Chicago: Moody Press, 1980), 2:597-598, **innocent** (#1412b).
8. *Strong's, bar* #H1249.
9. Harris, **purge** (#288).
10. *Vine's,* p. 103.
11. *Vine's,* p. 103.
12. *Strong's,* #G3700.
13. *Strong's,* #G3708.

Chapter 5

A Loving Heart

And thou shalt love the Lord thy God with all thine heart, and with all thy soul, and with all thy might (Deuteronomy 6:5).

What is love? There is probably no person alive above the age of 15 who has not asked that question. It is an age-old question that spans the centuries and crosses all cultural, racial, and social boundaries. Understanding love has been the quest of philosophers, poets, songwriters, novelists, romantics, and religious leaders throughout the ages. The world is obsessed with unraveling loves mysteries, plumbing the depths of its motivations, and soaring the heights of its joys. Perhaps because it is so rare in the world, true love is valued more highly than riches, houses, or lands. Many are the stories in man's heritage of people who gave up all these and more in order to find genuine love, the kind of love that lasts forever.

Unfortunately, our world is starved for true love. This is true first of all because it doesn't understand it, and second of all because it doesn't know where to find it. Humanity's understanding of love became distorted when Adam and Eve sinned in the Garden of Eden. Before their fall they were complete in each other, looking out for each other in selfless giving—the very essence of love. After their disobedience they began to look inward at themselves. Their outlook became essentially selfish. As a result, much of what the world calls "love" is really lust, the selfish desire to gratify one's own flesh even at the expense of other people, especially those who are the objects of that "love." Here is the essential difference: love gives, lust takes; love is self*less*, lust is self*ish*. It is no wonder that the world has trouble understanding love.

Because the world does not understand true love, it does not know where to find it either. My own life is a good illustration of this. I was a band leader and professional musician for over 26 years, many of them as an unbeliever. During that time I sang hundreds of love songs to thousands of people, yet their life was not changed. Neither was mine. As a lost sinner in need of salvation I was looking for love in all the wrong places. Many times I thought I had found it, but to no avail.

A turning point in my life came when my first wife was shot and killed. My second wife died of cancer. By that time I had given my heart to Jesus, but I was still young and immature in the faith. I had many heartaches, struggles, and trouble within my family. There were many times when I simply wanted to die. More than once I thought of taking my own life. God's love was in my heart, however, and each time He sustained me and brought me through. God's love was the only power that kept me alive. In His love God brought into my life a third wife, Lezlie, a great woman of God through whom I learned new levels of love, both for God and in human relationships. I gradually learned more about love— true love, the God-kind of love—even as I began to realize that God had greater plans for me.

In Christ I found kindness and set aside confusion; I found compassion and set aside adversity. I have learned how to care and to share and how to give up selfishness and hardheadedness. The love of God brought me out of spiritual darkness into the light of real life. When God saved me, He totally rearranged my life and made it new. As I sought to understand more of this new love that was now in my life, God revealed to me that I couldn't really understand true love because my own heart was not right before Him. Humbled and repentant, I waited before the Lord. He then showed me that *true love must come from the heart* and that *pure love comes only from a pure heart.* He told me that this is a truth that many people, including many Christians, do not understand.

If we want to understand true love and know what it means to have a loving heart, expressing pure love toward God and men, we must first understand the nature and depth of the love that comes to us from the very heart of God Himself.

Love From the Heart of God

If everything that has ever been written about love was gathered together and laid side-by-side, the line would probably encircle the globe. Human writers and artists have produced many wonderful and sublime expressions of love through the ages, but even the greatest of them do not equal the love book given by God Himself. The Bible, still the number one bestseller throughout the world, is the greatest love story ever told: the story of God's eternal love affair with mankind.

From the very first page the love of God shines forth, so vast and deep, so tender and complete that it reaches beyond human wisdom, knowledge, and understanding. God's love cuts through the mind, the spirit, and the flesh, reaching into the secret, precious inner self—the hidden man of the heart where his treasures are kept. God's love for us is evident throughout the Scriptures, not only in what He says, but also in what He does. Consider these words from Jeremiah:

> *The Lord hath appeared of old unto me, saying, Yea, I* **have loved thee with an everlasting love: therefore with lovingkindness have I drawn thee** (Jeremiah 31:3).

The Hebrew word translated "loved" is *ahab*, the basic expression in Hebrew meaning "to love." It is equivalent to the English word in the sense that it means a "strong emotional attachment to and desire either to possess or to be in the presence of the object"[1] of that love. So when God says that He loves us, it means He has a strong desire to possess us as His own and to be in fellowship with us. The word translated "love" is *ahabah*; it is the noun form of *ahab* and has the same meaning.

"Everlasting" is *olam*, which means "eternity; remotest time; perpetuity"[2] and "indefinite continuance into the very distant future."[3] God's desire to be our God and to be in fellowship with us never changes; it is constant.

"Lovingkindness" is a translation of the Hebrew *checed* (*hesed*), a word that is "one of the most important in the vocabulary of Old Testament theology and ethics."[4] It has three basic meanings, which always interact: "strength," "steadfastness," and "love." Proper understanding of the word involves all three of these ideas.[5] *Checed* "refers primarily to mutual and reciprocal rights and obligations between the parties of a relationship...[and] implies personal involvement...beyond the rule of law."[6] In His love, God has initiated a relationship with us in which He promises His love, strength, and steadfastness. Our part is to be faithful and obedient to Him. It is a relationship governed by *love*, not *law*.

God is true to His promises. It can be no other way. In Hebrews 6:13-14 we are told that when God makes a promise, He swears by *Himself* because there is no greater authority. God puts His very nature and integrity on the line. Therefore, when God says to us, "I love you," we can be sure that He means it. From the beginning of time God has continually manifested His love to all creation. He has kept on loving even when His love has been rejected. Love is the very heart of God's nature: "And we have known and believed the love that God hath to us. *God is love*; and *he that dwelleth in love dwelleth in God*, and God in him" (1 Jn. 4:16). God loves every one of us from His heart.

The greatest expression of God's love from the heart is Jesus. The very manifestation of God's love, Jesus was the perfect image and representation of the Father (see Heb. 1:3). God proved His love for us when He sent His Son to die on the cross to save us from our sins and to bring us back to Himself. This is clear throughout the New Testament: "*For God so loved the world, that He gave His only begotten Son,* that whosoever believeth in Him should not perish, but have everlasting life" (Jn. 3:16); "This is My commandment, That ye love one another, as *I have loved you. Greater love hath no man than this, that a man lay down his life for his friends*" (Jn. 15:12-13); "But *God commendeth His love toward us,* in that, while we were yet sinners, *Christ died for us*" (Rom. 5:8).

The most important truth concerning Christ's birth, ministry, death, and resurrection is the demonstration of His love for all mankind. Jesus not only showed us what love is, He also taught us how to love. It is His love in us that allows us to show kindness to our neighbors. This kind of love comes only through intimate relationship with the Lord, who is the very essence of love. Every believer must develop a love relationship with Him that is *from the heart.* As First John 4:16 says, if we dwell in love, we dwell in God. If we love the Lord *from our heart,* we will dwell with Him forever.

God-Style Love

God's love is a kind not naturally found in our sin-fallen and sin-filled world. It is a divine love found only in Him and in the heart of believers who have been remade in His image and likeness through the death and resurrection of Christ and the indwelling presence of the Holy Spirit. This love is so unique, in fact, that the usual human words for love are inadequate to express it.

In the New Testament, the Greek verb *agapao*, "to love," and the equivalent noun *agape*, "love," were used to refer to this one-of-a-kind God-style love. These two words are the most characteristic terms that describe or define Christianity.[7] Although the words themselves are not completely unique to the New Testament, the meanings attached to them there are. The Spirit of biblical revelation inspired the New Testament writers to use *agapao* and *agape* to "express ideas previously unknown."[8] These words describe God's attitude toward His Son, toward the human race in general, and, in particular, toward those who believe in Jesus Christ as Lord. They also express His will to us as believers concerning our attitudes toward each other and toward all people.[9] These same words are used to express the proper attitude of heart and mind that we as believers are to have toward the Lord. We are to love Him the way He loves us as He puts that love in our heart.

Put another way, *agapao* and *agape* express...

"the deep and *constant* 'love' and interest of a perfect Being towards entirely unworthy objects, producing and fostering a *reverential 'love'* in them towards the Giver, and a practical 'love' towards those who are partakers of the same, and a desire to help others to seek the Giver."[10]

God pours out His love (*agape*) on us even though we do not deserve it. When we respond and accept His love, it produces in us a like kind of love for Him, which expresses itself in the same kind of love for other believers in particular and all people in general.

Agape is a love of action, being completely selfless and giving and expending itself for the complete and total good of the object of that love. The greatest example of this is Jesus' death on the cross. Jesus gave Himself completely for us. He expended Himself for us that we might be saved—a perfect expression of *agape* in action. This is truly the "greater love" that causes one to "lay down his life for his friends" (see Jn. 15:13).

In chapter 13 of First Corinthians, the apostle Paul gave what is undoubtedly the highest and most sublime description of *agape* found anywhere:

> *Love suffers long and is kind; love does not envy; love does not parade itself, is not puffed up; does not behave rudely, does not seek its own, is not provoked, thinks no evil; does not rejoice in iniquity, but rejoices in the truth; bears all things, believes all things, hopes all things, endures all things. Love never fails. But whether there are prophecies, they will fail; whether there are tongues, they will cease; whether there is knowledge, it will vanish away....And now abide faith, hope, love, these three; but the greatest of these is love* (1 Corinthians 13:4-8,13 NKJ).

Paul said that love is the greatest of the spiritual gifts given to believers. Our life should be characterized by the qualities of love listed here. Because this love originates with God and comes only from Him, these qualities also describe God's love for us. As God loves us from His heart and pours out His *agape* on us, so we also should love God and one another from our heart, letting God's *agape* flow from us to others through the power of the Spirit. An old song says, "What the world needs now is love, sweet love." What the world needs is not just *any* love, but *agape*, the unique God-style love that He has spread abroad in the lives of His people. We must share that love with a world that is desperately crying out for it.

If there is so much love in the Church, how can there be so much hate and division between denominations? We have perfect doctrine, perfect churches, perfect sermons, and perfect songs, but do we have perfect hearts? No. A perfect heart must be laden with perfect love.

Covenant of Love

Wherever love dwells God dwells, because God is love. From the beginning God has desired to fellowship with His children and to dwell in our midst. That was the condition in the Garden of Eden before the fall. Adam and Eve enjoyed perfect fellowship with each other and with God. That fellowship was broken by sin, but God sought to restore it and to bring man back to Himself.

In love God chose Abraham and established a covenant with him to make of him a mighty nation that would bless all the people of the world. In love God led Isaac and Jacob and built a great people just as He had promised Abraham. In love God raised up Moses and delivered His people from slavery in Egypt. In love He led them to Mt. Sinai, where He gave them the Ten Commandments and the rest of the Law to teach them how to be His people. In love God provided for them in the wilderness even when their rebellion denied them entrance into the Promised Land for 40 years. In love God led the Israelites by the hand of Joshua into the land and established them as a nation. In love He raised up wise and godly leaders such as David and Solomon. When the people sinned and turned away from God, in love He raised up prophets like Isaiah, Jeremiah, and Elijah to warn them and call them back to Him.

God's love has always been a powerful covering that has protected and led His people. In Egypt, when the Israelites obeyed God by spreading lamb's blood on the doorposts of their house, God in His love caused the death angel to "pass over" and preserve them while every home of the Egyptians suffered the deaths of their firstborn. During the Babylonian exile, Daniel was faithful to pray to God three times a day. He loved God so much that when he was thrown into the lion's den, God shut the lion's mouths and protected Daniel. God's love covered him. When Shadrach, Meshach, and Abednego were thrown into the fiery furnace for refusing to dishonor

God with idolatry, He met them there. Not one of their bones was broken, neither did their clothes burn or their hair singe. Love walked with them in the fire. Love took the heat out of the flames. They came out of the furnace intact and unharmed.

Abraham, Isaac, and Jacob were men of God's love. Moses, Joshua, David, and Solomon were men of God's love. Isaiah, Jeremiah, and Elijah were men of God's love. Daniel, Shadrach, Meshach, and Abednego were men of God's love. The pages of the Old Testament are filled with such stories that defy human understanding—stories of an incredible love relationship that existed between God and men, stories of people who knew both *the love of God* and *the God of love.*

Yet we who are believers today have a better love covenant than they had. The covenant of the Law was written on tablets of stone. It contained the great love principle, but not the power to enable sinful people to live by that love. With the coming of Jesus the covenant is no longer written on cold, hard stone; rather it is written on warm, living hearts: "Forasmuch as ye are manifestly declared to be the epistle of Christ ministered by us, written not with ink, but with the Spirit of the living God; not in tables of stone, but in fleshly tables of the heart" (2 Cor. 3:3). We have the complete Word of God— the Holy Spirit lives in us and God's laws are written on our hearts—whereas the men and women of old had only a *promised* love covenant sealed by the blood of a lamb. We have a living, fulfilled, *completed* love covenant sealed by the blood of Jesus, the Lamb of God.

We who have been washed in His blood and baptized in His name now await a final heavenly calling. We are heirs of God, priests of God, and kings unto God—ambassadors of His glory, righteousness, and love.

Love From Our Heart

The heart of the covenant between God and man— whether old or new—is this: "Thou shalt love the Lord thy

God with all thine heart, and with all thy soul, and with all thy might" (Deut. 6:5). Jesus said that this was the first and greatest commandment and that on it, along with the commandment to love our neighbors as ourselves, hung the Law and the prophets (see Mt. 22:37-40). In other words, the fulfillment of God's Word in our life centers around our loving Him with our whole being—body, mind, and spirit (the hidden man of the heart wherein is stored all our treasures from God)—and through that love, loving others in His name and seeking to bring them into the experience of His love for themselves.

If God's *agape* is so powerful, why don't we see more evidence of it in our daily lives and in our churches? In large part, it is because we have allowed our heart to become dirty, impure, and divided, making us out of fellowship with the Lord. Our heart is like a dirty mirror that reflects only a poor and partial image. We have become like streams of water that are clogged with dirt, rocks, tree limbs, and dead leaves so that only a tiny trickle can pass through. Our heart is not right before God, so our love is not right. Something has gotten "out of kilter."

As a pastor I have seen many people come into the church shouting and giving God praise. Unfortunately, the heart condition of these folks didn't always agree with their outward expression, and the insufficient supply of love flowing into and out of their heart soon caused them to suffer a spiritual stroke and leave the church. Love is the way we as believers identify with and relate to God. Do you want to be closer to the Lord? Do you want to know Him, see His face, hear His voice, and feel His presence? The *only* way is to give Him your whole heart in love. Surrender your self-control; offer yourself completely to God and ask Him to fill you with His love and to help you love Him with all your heart.

Saints, we need to protect our heart to make sure that it doesn't become hardened. Love cannot dwell in a hardened heart. Humility and surrender in faith will break up the fallow ground of our heart and allow God's love to soak it and soften it until we are full of His love. God wants us to be full to overflowing with His love. Consider how Paul expressed it to the Ephesians:

> For this cause I bow my knees unto the Father of our Lord Jesus Christ, of whom the whole family in heaven and earth is named, **that He would grant you**, according to the riches of His glory, **to be strengthened with might by His Spirit in the inner man**; that Christ may dwell in your hearts by faith; that ye, **being rooted and grounded in love**, may be able to comprehend with all saints what is the breadth, and length, and depth, and height; and **to know the love of Christ**, which passeth knowledge, that ye might **be filled with all the fulness of God** (Ephesians 3:14-19).

When we come to God in humility and faith, He will strengthen our inner man through His Spirit, will ground us in His love, and will fill us with His fullness. We will then know from experience the love of Christ.

Love was Christ's motivation; let it be our motivation as well. Let us *pray* with love from our heart. Let us *preach* with love from our heart. Let us *teach* with love from our heart. Let us *work*, *give*, and *worship* the Lord with love from our heart. Whenever we say those precious words, "I love you," whether to God or man, let us say them from our heart. Otherwise our words are cheap and demeaning. We must not cheapen our love or let it grow cold and hard. Love from the heart is *unconditional*; there are no strings attached. God loves us because it is His nature to love and because He chooses to, not because we deserve it. Our love should be just as pure. Only by daily and continual surrender of our heart and will to God can we have this purity of love.

God's love in our heart will change the way we act, the way we talk, and the way we relate with our spouses, our children, our co-workers, our brothers and sisters in Christ, and our neighbors. Jesus said to His disciples, "A new commandment I give unto you, That ye love one another; as I have loved you, that ye also love one another. By this shall all men know that ye are My disciples, if ye have love one to another" (Jn. 13:34-35). The love of Christ in us is the greatest single proof we have to show the world that He is real. Having the love of Christ in us means that we will walk in love even when people lie about us, cheat us, steal from us, try to push us aside, or in any other way revile us, persecute us, or say all manner of evil against us falsely. Through every trial and tribulation we must show love to everyone whom we come in contact with. We must pray for those who despitefully use us and bless those who curse us. Love allows the hidden man of the heart to reveal himself to all, openly showing the treasures he keeps there. Love allows the most wretched sinner to know God.

To know God is to love God. To love God is to love one another. To love one another is to love those outside the faith. To love those outside the faith is to walk in love to bring them in. I think John expressed this interlinked love relationship well when he wrote:

> **Beloved, let us love one another: for love is of God;** and every one that loveth is born of God, and knoweth God. He that loveth not knoweth not God; for **God is love.** In this was manifested the love of God toward us, because that God sent His only begotten Son into the world, that we might live through Him. **Herein is love, not that we loved God, but that He loved us,** and sent His Son to be the propitiation for our sins. **Beloved, if God so loved us, we ought also to love one another.** No man hath seen God at any time. **If we love one another, God dwelleth in us, and His love is perfected in us** (1 John 4:7-12).

Saints, we need to give our heart anew to our Lord and let Him perfect His love in us. God's love in our heart brings balance to our life and fixes our commitment firmly on Him. It sets the tone of our heart, mind, and spirit. Love from the heart helps us make a new start and gives us a new outlook on life. It enables us to see the world through God's eyes.

Our world cries out in need of knowing God and His love through Jesus Christ His Son. As Christians we are Christ's ambassadors of love to a lost, dying, and love-starved world. God's love perfected in us will protect us, preserve us, and prepare us for Heaven; it will also send us out into our neighborhoods, cities, and nations to bring others into the loving embrace of the Father.

Endnotes

1. W.E. Vine, Merrill F. Unger, and William White, Jr. *Vine's Complete Expository Dictionary of Old and New Testament Words* (Nashville: Thomas Nelson Publishers, 1985), p. 141.
2. *Vine's*, p. 72.
3. R. Laird Harris, Gleason L. Archer, Jr., and Bruce K. Waltke, eds. *Theological Wordbook of the Old Testament* (Chicago: Moody Press, 1980), 2:672, **forever** (#1631a).
4. *Vine's*, p. 142.
5. *Vine's*, p. 142.
6. *Vine's*, p. 142.
7. *Vine's*, p. 381.
8. *Vine's*, p. 381.
9. *Vine's*, p. 381.
10. *Vine's*, p. 382.

Chapter 6

A Joyful Heart

Be glad in the Lord, and rejoice, ye righteous: and shout for joy, all ye that are upright in heart (Psalm 32:11).

A merry heart doeth good like a medicine: but a broken spirit drieth the bones (Proverbs 17:22).

It's Sunday morning. You wake up ready to go, well-rested and full of energy. Your pastor has been urging everyone to be on time for church, so you hurry to get ready, your excitement growing by the minute. As you wind your way through the morning traffic you notice what a beautiful day it is. It seems as though the sun has never been so bright, the sky so blue, or the fragrance of the flowers so sweet on the morning dew. A hymn that you heard earlier on a Christian radio station plays itself over and over in your mind. You feel absolutely wonderful! What a great thing it is to be saved!

The church sanctuary is more crowded than usual but you hardly notice. You have come to worship God. As you take your seat, the choir begins to sing one of your favorite songs. The presence of God is so real, so strong to you. As worship progresses, your mind turns to thoughts of how good God has been to you, how far He has brought you. As you consider what you might have become if He hadn't rescued you from sin, you realize anew that—glory be to God—you are not the person you once were. Spontaneously, unbidden words of praise to God form on your lips.

Something wells up from deep within your spirit: a warm rush of emotion, an overwhelming sense of well-being that consumes you. You cannot remain silent. Praise and rejoicing bubble forth from your mouth. You find that you can't keep still. You raise your hands. Your feet begin to move, almost of their own accord. You remember the day the doctors gave you no hope—but Jesus healed you. You can never forget the day He pulled you out of the terrible pit of sin.

Unable to sit still any longer, you rise to your feet. Some of the other worshipers give you strange looks; you pay them no heed. They don't know all that God has done for you. The pastor doesn't know; the deacons and ushers don't know. No one but you knows the depth of God's goodness, love, and blessings to you.

Now your legs are moving as though they had a mind of their own. You rush into the center aisle where—to the astonishment of the pastor, the choir, the deacons, your friends, your family, and the rest of the congregation—you begin to dance before the Lord! It is not a rehearsed or a learned dance, but a spontaneous outpouring of the joy that floods your heart; it is a joy unspeakable and unquenchable, given to you by the God who loves you so much.

Afraid to Be Happy

In many of our churches today such a free and open expression of praise, worship, and joy would result in your being hastily escorted out the nearest door and asked never to return. It wouldn't matter that you never stepped on anyone's toes or fell over a pew or in any other way acted indecently or out of order. It wouldn't make any difference that you were trying to give expression to the inexpressible joy bubbling up in your spirit. Unrestrained joy makes many church people nervous. Why?

Why are so many churches afraid of happiness, particularly in worship? Of course, very few pastors or other church leaders would ever say that they did not want the members of their churches to be happy. Yet most churches have standards or traditions, some written but (mostly) unwritten, that define the limits of "acceptable" behavior. Some churches allow and encourage great freedom of movement and expression with raised hands and dancing; others accept raised hands as long as you stay put in your pew, but dancing is *absolutely* out of the question! At the other end are the churches that discourage any and all such outward displays of emotion. Most churches fall somewhere in between. When it comes to expressions of joy and excitement in worship, it's as though we say, "This far, but no farther!" What are we afraid of?

As Christians we should welcome joy and embrace it as a precious gift from a loving God. Joy is what sets us apart from the rest of the world. Our God is a God of joy. The Bible says that God Himself rejoices over His people: "The Lord thy God in the midst of thee is mighty; He will save, He will rejoice over thee with joy; He will rest in His love, He will joy over thee with singing" (Zeph. 3:17). The God of joy wants His children to be people of joy.

The world as a whole expends most of its time, energy, and resources in a desperate, never-ending search for happiness. Most people are willing to do *anything* that they believe holds the promise or even just the possibility of true happiness. Some seek it in drugs or alcohol; others in money or sex. Many try to find it in religion (empty traditions, rituals, and creeds rather than a love relationship with God). The "joy" the world offers in all these things and more is a cruel deception; it is satan's counterfeit. True joy is not found in the world or in the things of the world. True joy comes *from the heart of God*.

No matter how far we travel in the world or how hard we look, we will never find the Spirit of joy apart from giving our heart to Jesus Christ. Joy is a fruit of the Spirit (see Gal. 5:22), who releases it into our inner man, where all the hidden treasures of the heart are found.

Inspired singing, powerful preaching, anointed teaching— any of these may be the spark that releases joy within us. Joy may also surprise us, popping up unexpectedly while we are driving down the highway, taking a shower, or shopping for groceries. Wherever and whenever it happens, joy is to be embraced with gratitude, even while we remember that joy and praise are natural for God's children: "Rejoice in the Lord, O ye righteous: for praise is comely for the upright" (Ps. 33:1). Don't ever be ashamed of your joy, regardless of your circumstances, condition, or position.

If you can't rejoice in church, where can you rejoice? It's really a shame that so many churches do not allow real liberty of joy and freedom of expression in worship. Dancing, lifting up holy hands, singing, shouting, running, leaping, speaking in tongues—all these are appropriate *as the Spirit leads*. If you don't feel true freedom of worship in your church, you may want to pray that the Spirit will open up your church more. However, it may be necessary to find another church, one that will allow and encourage you to give full expression to the joy you feel in your heart. We are not the authors of joy; God is. Therefore, when joy comes, we should honor God.

Now, certainly joy comes in many different packages. True joy is not always exuberant and boisterous; it does not always show itself in conspicuous external display. Sometimes joy is a quiet, warm intensity that brings tears to our eyes; other times it is an irresistible sense of well-being that brings a smile to our face and a lightness to our step. True joy is determined by its source, not its appearance. No matter how it manifests itself, true joy always comes from God.

Nevertheless, many churches are scared of joy. If you manifest it you may be banned from the pew, the deacon board, or even the pulpit. You may be accused of "disorderly conduct." What a shame (for those churches). Don't despair. Set yourself to follow the Spirit in everything you do, and He will lead you. Remember the words of the proverb: "Trust in the Lord with all thine heart; and lean not unto thine own understanding. In all thy ways acknowledge Him, and He shall direct thy paths" (Prov. 3:5-6). A joyful Christian is a stable Christian. A joyful Christian is a fruitful Christian. *Never* be afraid or ashamed to praise the Lord or to let out the joy that's in your heart!

Created for Joy

The joy of the Lord is something that the world can neither give nor understand. With its origin in the heart of God, it is spiritual in nature. Therefore it is beyond the comprehension of those who are outside the Spirit of God. This is what the apostle Paul meant when he wrote to the Corinthians that the natural man (the lost world) could neither receive nor understand the things of the Spirit because they are spiritually discerned (see 1 Cor. 2:14). Yet we who are believers can both receive and understand joy because "we have the mind of Christ" (1 Cor. 2:16b). God's Spirit dwelling in us shapes us into ready receptacles of His joy. This presence of God's joy in us is a partial restoration of the conditions that existed in Eden before the fall.

God is a God of joy, and He created us to be joyful. The first chapter of Genesis uses the phrase "it was good" six times to indicate God's attitude toward His creation (verses 4,10,12,18,21,25). After the creation of man and the completion of His creative activity, God saw that all He had made was "very good" (verse 31). In each of these seven instances the Hebrew word for "good" is *towb*, which, besides its basic meaning of "good" in the widest sense, also means "cheerful," "joyful," and "merry."[1] Joy was at the very heart of creation, including man.

In the beginning, Adam and Eve walked in joyful relationship with each other and with God. Joy filled their days, their nights, their conversation, and everything they did. They were in perfect harmony with God and with all the created order. Everything was as it should be. When sin was born, however, joy died. Sin broke the relationship, destroyed the fellowship, and killed the spirit of man. Joy was gone, and ever since then the quest to bring it back has consumed the resources, energy, and imagination of man.

What man cannot restore, God can. The breach in man's relationship with God caused by sin has been repaired in Christ. The cross of Calvary bridges the gap. Repentance and confession of sin open the door for faith unto salvation to be implanted in the heart. Faith, once established, conditions the heart to receive joy.

Joy is a natural result of being brought into a right relationship with God. It is one of the blessings of salvation. Consider these Scriptures: "Therefore with joy shall ye draw water out of the wells of salvation" (Is. 12:3); "Yet I will rejoice in the Lord, I will joy in the God of my salvation" (Hab. 3:18); "And my soul shall be joyful in the Lord: it shall rejoice in His salvation" (Ps. 35:9).When King David was under deep conviction for his sins that had disrupted his fellowship with God and robbed him of joy, he cried out, "Restore unto me the joy of Thy salvation; and uphold me with Thy free spirit" (Ps. 51:12).

Joy is a *birthright* for children of God. He expects, even commands, us to rejoice as a way of life: "Be glad in the Lord, and rejoice, ye righteous: and shout for joy, all ye that are upright in heart" (Ps. 32:11); "But let all those that put their trust in thee rejoice: let them ever shout for joy, because Thou defendest them: let them also that love Thy name be joyful in Thee" (Ps. 5:11); "Glory ye in His holy name: let the heart of them rejoice that seek the Lord" (1 Chron. 16:10); "Rejoice, and be exceeding glad: for great is your reward in heaven..." (Mt. 5:12).

Jesus Himself was concerned about our joy. He said to His disciples, "These things have I spoken unto you, that My joy might remain in you, and that your joy might be full" (Jn. 15:11). A little later He prayed to His Father: "And now come I to Thee; and these things I speak in the world, that they [His disciples] might have My joy fulfilled in themselves" (Jn. 17:13).

It should be clear then that a joyful heart is God's will and purpose for His people. Through the death and resurrection of His Son, God has restored the joy lost at the fall. Now He wants believers everywhere to "rejoice evermore" (1 Thess. 5:16) because of the reborn relationship with Him that Christ accomplished for us at Calvary. If we are not exhibiting joy in our life or our churches, we are not fulfilling God's complete purpose and plan for us. If we lack joy, we need to examine ourselves to see if there is sin in our heart. Sin will disrupt our fellowship with God and steal our joy (as David discovered; see Psalm 51). Confession and repentance will restore both fellowship and joy (as David also discovered; see Psalm 32).

So my brother, my sister, all who claim the name of Jesus, *rejoice in the Lord!* Let His joy well up in you and spill out in praise, worship, and service, touching others so they too can know His joy. *Be joyful in God!* It's what He created you to be!

Joy—A Heart Medicine

It is a well-attested fact that happy, joy-filled people tend to live longer and experience less illness; and when they *do* get sick, they recover more quickly than unhappy people do. There is a definite link between wellness and a positive outlook on life, between joy and good health. The saints of old knew this to be true. The writer of the Book of Proverbs said, "A merry heart doeth good like a medicine: but a broken spirit drieth the bones" (Prov. 17:22). How we need to hear and heed that simple truth today! Our hospitals and mental institutions are filled with people whose spirits are broken and whose hearts are joyless.

"Heart" in this verse is the Hebrew *leb*, which, as we discussed in Chapter 1, is the basic Hebrew word for "heart" but is also used to refer to the center of anything, and especially to the feelings, the will, and the intellect.[2] The Hebrew word translated "merry" is *sameach*, which could also be rendered "gleeful," "glad," "joyful," or "rejoicing."[3] "Doeth good" is from *yatab*, which has the basic meaning of "to make well."[4] *Nake* ("broken") also means "afflicted," "stricken," and "wounded,"[5] while *yabesh* ("drieth") can also mean "to wither away."[6] One way to paraphrase Proverbs 17:22 would be, "Joy makes your heart well like a medicine, but a wounded spirit will cause you to wither away."

Joy comes from the Lord. Joy strengthens the heart, and a strong heart is a healthy heart. Scripture teaches us that the *joy of the Lord* is our strength (see Neh. 8:10). King David wrote, "*The Lord is my strength* and my shield; *my heart trusted in Him*, and I am helped: therefore *my heart greatly rejoiceth*; and with my song will I praise Him" (Ps. 28:7). Asaph, another psalmist, wrote, "My flesh and my heart faileth: but *God is the strength of my heart*, and my portion for ever" (Ps. 73:26).

Joy drives out sorrow, sadness, depression, and loneliness. It can restore marriages, renew friendships, and solidify our relationship with God. Joy causes us to prosper and to be in good health; it gives us a peace the world cannot offer. A joyful heart will keep you from backsliding. It will help you resist and flee temptation. Joy makes you strong and keeps you strong.

I have witnessed devils driven out by the presence of joy. I have seen people healed of their diseases and delivered from drugs, alcohol, and other addictions and bad habits by the presence of joy. I have seen people receive the gift of the Holy Spirit by the presence of joy.

Are you sick, spiritually anemic, with a heart weak from a joy deficiency? Is a broken spirit withering you away? Take time to reflect on the goodness of God and the greatness of His love. The joy of the Lord is a great restorative. Let Him apply the medicine of His joy to your hurting heart. Let Him rub the healing balm of a merry disposition into your wounded spirit.

Joy Prepares Us for Heaven

It is important that as believers we learn to experience and express joy here on earth because all the activity of Heaven will be permeated with joy. The holy joy that stirs our heart here serves to prepare us for the joy of Heaven. The Bible promises that there will be no sorrow or suffering in Heaven (see Rev. 21:3-4). However, the more we learn to practice joy here, the fuller and richer our joy will be there. The more we learn to walk in His joy on earth, the fuller our enjoyment of Heaven will be.

There is joy in the presence of the Lord. One of David's psalms says, "Thou wilt show me the path of life: *in Thy presence is fulness of joy*; at Thy right hand there are pleasures for evermore" (Ps. 16:11). Paul asked of the Thessalonians, "For what is our hope, or joy, or crown of rejoicing? Is it not even you in the presence of our Lord Jesus Christ at His coming?" (1 Thess. 2:19 NKJ) Even the angels of Heaven rejoice. Jesus said, "Likewise, I say unto you, there is joy in the presence of the angels of God over one sinner that repenteth" (Lk. 15:10).

Joy is serious business in Heaven! In fact, it is one of the pillars of the divine realm. Paul wrote to the Romans, "For *the kingdom of God* is not meat and drink; but *righteousness,* and *peace,* and *joy* in the Holy Ghost" (Rom. 14:17). Jesus endured the cross because of the joy to come: "Looking unto Jesus the author and finisher of our faith; *who for the joy that was set before Him endured the cross,* despising the shame, and is set down at the right hand of the throne of God" (Heb. 12:2).

What a time of rejoicing we will have in God's presence when we see Him face to face! We can't even begin to imagine in this life what the joy of Heaven will be like. Consider Paul's words to the Corinthians: "But as it is written, Eye hath not seen, nor ear heard, neither have entered into the heart of man, the things which God hath prepared for them that love Him" (1 Cor. 2:9). When we get to Heaven, our joy will be complete because we will be like Jesus, who is our joy: "Beloved, now are we the sons of God, and it doth not yet appear what we shall be: but we know that, when He shall appear, we shall be like Him; for we shall see Him as He is" (1 Jn. 3:2). There will be no gravity to hold us down and no tiredness, aches, or pains to trouble our new bodies. No one will tell us to sit down. With the countless thousands of saints and angels we will rejoice around the throne of God!

I'm afraid that those who believe only in "holy quietness" may be very uncomfortable in Heaven. The entirety of creation will be shouting for joy! What a day it will be! What a glorious day that will be! Let's get ready for it now! Let's loose ourselves from the traditions that bind us. "Let us lay aside every weight, and the sin which doth so easily beset us..." (Heb. 12:1b); let's get free from anything and everything that hinders the free expression of our joy.

Saints, we were created for joy. It is a medicine to our spirits. Let's not waste time. Let us heed the words of the apostle Paul: "Rejoice in the Lord alway: and again I say, Rejoice" (Phil. 4:4)!

Endnotes

1. James Strong, *Strong's Exhaustive Concordance of the Bible* (Peabody, MA: Hendrickson Publishers, n.d.), #H2896.
2. *Strong's*, #H3820.
3. *Strong's*, #H8056.
4. *Strong's*, #H3190.
5. *Strong's*, #H5218.
6. *Strong's*, #H3001.

Chapter 7

A Peaceful Heart

Thou wilt keep him in perfect peace, whose mind is stayed on Thee: because he trusteth in Thee (Isaiah 26:3).

And let the peace of God rule in your hearts, to the which also ye are called in one body; and be ye thankful (Colossians 3:15).

Normal heart function involves a two-phase process of contraction and relaxation: the systolic and the diastolic. In the systolic phase the heart contracts, pumping blood throughout the body. During the diastolic phase the heart completely relaxes and expands as blood fills its chambers and is reheated in preparation for the next systole (contraction). In a healthy heart this cycle is repeated tirelessly and continuously second by second, minute by minute, hour by hour, day after day, year after year: contracting, relaxing; pumping, resting. The average heart beats 100,000 times a day and pumps 2,000 gallons of blood through the body. During an average 70-year lifetime, the heart will beat more than 2.5 billion times[1] and pump over 50 million gallons of blood.

The diastolic phase of rest is just as important as the systolic phase of contraction. If the heart does not relax between beats, it can neither fill up with blood again properly nor pump blood adequately. Some types of heart failure and other coronary problems are caused by a condition called diastolic dysfunction, where the heart does not relax completely. Therefore, it is harder for blood to enter the heart, and increased pressure and fluid in the blood vessels of the lungs or in the ones returning to the heart can be the result.[2] A healthy life thus depends just as much on the heart *resting* at the proper time as it does on the heart *working* at the proper time.

This principle of rest is also important where the spiritual heart is concerned. A heart at rest has the strength to do its work. A heart at rest is a heart at *peace*. Lack of peace in our heart negatively affects everything else. We can't relate rightly to God or to anyone else if our heart is in turmoil. Lack of peace robs us of our joy, destroys our confidence, and unsettles our sense of assurance regarding where we stand with God. (And our stand with God may be determined by the peace levels we have in Christ!)

Essentially, there are two kinds of peace: that which the world gives and that which comes only from God. The world's "peace" is a false peace because it generally focuses on external circumstances: absence of war or strife, surface quiet or tranquillity, or "civil" behavior between people. Any of these can mask unrest, fear, hostility, or anger that is lying just beneath the surface. As long as the external circumstances prevail, a sense of "peace" is felt. When those circumstances go away, however, so does the sense of peace. There is no true, lasting peace available from the world.

God's peace, on the other hand, is a lasting peace because it is based on spiritual truth—on the very nature of God Himself—rather than on physical circumstances. Because it is spiritual in nature, this peace is beyond the world's understanding. This is why Jesus said to His disciples, "Peace I leave with you, *My peace I give unto you: not as the world giveth,* give I unto you. Let not your heart be troubled, neither let it be afraid" (Jn. 14:27). The Greek word for "peace" is *eirene,* which also means "one," "quietness," "rest," and "to set at one again."[3] In this verse it particularly refers to "the harmonized relationships between God and man" and "the sense of rest and contentment consequent thereon."[4] All who are grounded and nourished by God's peace have been set at one with Him again and are in harmony with Him. They will not be shaken even when external circumstances change.

A believing heart that is pure before the Lord and filled with love and joy will also be a peaceful heart, knowing divine peace in two dimensions: peace *with* God and the peace *of* God. Before we can know the peace *of* God, however, we must have peace *with* God.

Peace With God

Ever since Adam and Eve ate the forbidden fruit in the Garden of Eden, the human race has been at enmity with God. We have insisted on going our own way, fashioning for ourselves "gods" made in our own likeness, and rejecting the God of the universe. Mankind is at war with God. There is no peace, nor can there be, at least from our side. We are hopelessly at odds with God.

God, however, was not caught by surprise over our rebellion. He loves us, and even before creation He established a plan by which we could be restored to a state of peace with Him. Consider Paul's words:

> *Blessed be the God and Father of our Lord Jesus Christ, who hath blessed us with all spiritual blessings in heavenly places in Christ: according as He hath chosen us in Him before the foundation of the world, that we should be holy and without blame before Him in love* (Ephesians 1:3-4).

God's plan called for the death of His Son for the sin and rebellion of man. Revelation 13:8 refers to Jesus as "the Lamb slain from the foundation of the world." In the heart and mind of God, Jesus, the Lamb of God, died for our sins *before the foundation of the world.*

We can have peace with God because He wills it to be so and has taken the initiative to do everything necessary to make it possible. Paul explained it this way:

> *Therefore being justified by faith,* **we have peace with God through our Lord Jesus Christ:** *by whom also we have access by faith into this grace wherein we stand, and rejoice in hope of the glory of God* (Romans 5:1-2).

Being justified means that we have been put into a right relationship with God. Faith is the instrument through which our justification is put into effect. Jesus said, "Thy faith hath saved thee" (see Lk. 7:50; 18:42), and Paul told the Ephesians, "For by grace are ye saved through faith..." (Eph. 2:8). Through this same faith we stand in the state of God's grace—His unmerited favor—and have the assurance of seeing and sharing in His glory as His redeemed children. All this has been made possible *through* the death and resurrection *of our Lord Jesus Christ.* The end result is *peace with God.*

Peace with God means being right with Him by having our sins forgiven and by living under His undeserved favor. We obtain peace with God when we confess our sins to Him and, in repentance, turn from our sins to God, placing our faith and trust in Jesus Christ as our Savior and giving Him control as Lord of our life. Jesus then sends the Holy Spirit to dwell in our heart, imparting His peace to us and making it possible for us to live in a way that honors God. A peaceful heart, then, is first of all a heart surrendered in faith to Jesus Christ unto salvation through the forgiveness of sins. Once we have peace *with* God in our heart, we are prepared to receive the peace *of* God.

The Peace of God

Having the peace *of* God is not the same as having peace *with* God, nor is it automatic just because we are saved. Peace *with* God applies to our eternal position with God, whereas the peace *of* God relates to the quality of our daily walk as believers. We can have peace *with* God where our salvation is concerned and yet lack the peace *of* God when we fail to walk in the Spirit. Peace is a fruit of the Spirit (see Gal. 5:22) and is available in full abundance to faithful believers who are living in obedience to the Lord. The peace of God is a calm assurance—an unshakable conviction of the absolute security of our relationship with God—and a confident sense of well-being and tranquillity of spirit that is not dependent upon external circumstances. It's designed by God to rest in the heart of His people that we may walk in confidence before Him all the days of our life—without the fear, worry, and stress that tend to uproot God's heart protection plan for the hidden man.

There are many things that can keep the peace of God from bearing fruit in our heart: disobedience, lack of forgiveness, unbelief, bitterness, unresolved anger, impure or lustful thoughts of the mind or actions of the body, pursuit of the things of the world instead of the things of God—indeed all kind of unconfessed sin; the list is virtually endless. Many of our churches are full of strife, division, and resentment between members over offenses both real and imagined. We fight over little things that amount to nothing and allow bitterness to go unresolved. Many churches have become veritable war zones, while others have allowed sinful attitudes and practices to become entrenched. The problem is very serious. Satan has gotten a foothold in many churches and in the life of many saints, and we end up blindly playing his game, thereby grieving the Spirit of God and destroying our witness before the world. How can we tell a lost, strife-torn world about the

Prince of Peace when we have no peace in our own heart or in our churches?

What can we do? How do we restore and preserve the peace of God in our heart? I think Paul's instructions to the Philippians are relevant here:

> *Rejoice in the Lord alway: and again I say, Rejoice. Let your moderation be known unto all men. The Lord is at hand. Be careful for nothing; but in every thing by prayer and supplication with thanksgiving let your requests be made known unto God. And the* **peace of God**, *which passeth all understanding, shall keep your hearts and minds through Christ Jesus. Finally, brethren, whatsoever things are true, whatsoever things are honest, whatsoever things are just, whatsoever things are pure, whatsoever things are lovely, whatsoever things are of good report; if there be any virtue, and if there be any praise, think on these things* (Philippians 4:4-8).

Praise, prayer, and thanksgiving are powerful peace preservatives for the heart. When we are busy bragging on God and His greatness, lifting up petition and intercession to Him, and expressing our gratitude for His blessings, we have no time for the things that destroy peace. Besides, practicing these things trains our mind and spirit to live on a higher plane. I think this is exactly what Paul is getting at when he says to think on the things that are true, honest, just, pure, lovely, of good report, virtuous, and praiseworthy. Among other things, this means learning to keep our mind, thoughts, and words out of the gutter!

We need to devote our energies to those things that edify (build up) rather than those things that tear down; to those things that bring our mind and heart into line with the mind and heart of Christ. Paul wrote to the Romans, "Let us therefore follow after the things which make for peace, and things wherewith one may edify another" (Rom. 14:19), and to the

Corinthians of "bringing into captivity every thought to the obedience of Christ" (2 Cor. 10:5b). There should be no place in our life for thoughts, words, or actions that cut, belittle, demean, or tear down. Instead, we should pursue peace aggressively, seeking to encourage and promote harmony between one another in the unity of the Spirit.

As we commit ourselves to the pursuits that Paul lines out in Philippians 4:4-8, we will experience "the peace of God, which passeth all understanding" and which will "keep [our] hearts and minds through Christ Jesus" (Phil. 4:7). "Keep" translates the Greek word *phroureo*, which means to "guard," or more specifically to "mount guard as a sentinel," as in posting guards or spies at the city gates[5] to watch and protect the sleeping city. The peace of God protects our heart and mind in Christ!

In fact, God Himself has promised to guard us in peace as we trust Him. The prophet Isaiah wrote, "Thou wilt keep him in perfect peace, whose mind is stayed on Thee: because he trusteth in Thee" (Is. 26:3). When our mind is *stayed* on God (Heb. *camak*—"to lean upon or take hold of"[6]) and we *trust* in Him (Heb. *batach*—" 'to hie for refuge,' 'to be confident or sure,' 'secure' "[7]), He will *keep* us (Heb. *natsar*—"guard, protect, preserve"[8]) in *perfect peace* (Heb. *shalowm*— " 'welfare,' 'health, prosperity,' 'rest' "[9]). The peace of God, a gift of His grace, is ours as we yield ourselves to Him and depend on Him for life and direction.

Called to Peace

By nature and calling we who claim the name of Christ are peacemakers. It is one of the characteristic traits that most identifies us as the people of God. Jesus said, "Blessed are the peacemakers: for they shall be called the children of God" (Mt. 5:9). Why are peacemakers called children of God? Our God is a God of peace. He is in the business of making peace both between Himself and lost, rebellious humanity, and

between men themselves. Children of God should act like
their Father. Peacemaking is godly work, so those who pursue
godly peace will be revealed to the world as children of the
God of peace.

Have we missed our calling of peace? Perhaps. Many of us
today who are believers are not very good peacemakers. Why?
Because we lack peace within ourselves. We are caught in a
whirlwind of worldly lifestyles that tosses us to and fro, leav-
ing us troubled, torn, tried, tired, and empty. Hurting in our
heart and vexed in our spirit, we need to remember that God
has established with us a *covenant of peace* that will remain
even when the physical world passes away:

> *For the mountains shall depart, and the hills be
> removed; but My kindness shall not depart from thee,*
> **neither shall the covenant of My peace be removed**,
> *saith the Lord that hath mercy on thee* (Isaiah 54:10).

> *Moreover **I will make a covenant of peace with them;
> it shall be an everlasting covenant with them: and I will
> place them, and multiply them**, and will set My sanctu-
> ary in the midst of them for evermore* (Ezekiel 37:26).

God's covenant of peace is a resting bond, the assurance of
everlasting quietness of spirit and holiness of heart. It is as
eternal as God Himself, and within its shelter we can fulfill
our calling as peacemakers in the world. When our heart is
right before God, His peace will rule us, fill us with thanksgiving, and bring us together in the unity of the Spirit. Consider Paul's words to the Colossians: "And *let the peace of
God rule in your hearts, to* the *which* also *ye are called* in one
body; and be ye thankful" (Col. 3:15).

The peace of God ruling in our heart will produce in our
life the fruit of peace, which then will be on display for all the
world to see. Our world longs for and desperately searches for
true peace but cannot find it because it is found only in Christ.
When the world sees the Church truly and openly manifesting

the fruit of peace, it will be pointed toward the God who is the author and giver of that peace. As lost people respond to the peace they see in us, many will turn to Christ in repentance and faith and receive from Him righteousness and peace in their own heart. As peacemakers, we sow seeds of peace in the world that bear the fruit of righteousness in changed lives. This is what James meant when he wrote, "Now the fruit of righteousness is sown in *peace* by those who make peace" (Jas. 3:18 NKJ).

Brethren, as Christians we have been called to a lifestyle of peace. By His death and resurrection Jesus Christ has brought us into peace with God. Through the Holy Spirit God has sown His peace in our heart where, as we follow and obey Him, it bears abundant fruit in our life and touches the life of others.

The Armor of Peace

Whether we like it or not, our hidden man must daily remain armed and ready for war, both outwardly and inwardly. As Christians in a sinful world we are in enemy territory, behind enemy lines. The same demonic forces of sin and evil that are at enmity with God are also at war with God's children. This is one reason why we face adversity in the world. In addition, we face an inward war between our old man—our sinful nature—and our new man—the hidden man of the heart that came to life when we were saved. Satan battles God to establish dominion over our inner man. God works to make our heart more heavenly, while satan tries to turn us more to the things and ways of the world.

Can there be peace in the midst of war? That depends on several things: the condition of our heart, the level of our preparation for battle, and the quality of our weapons. Soldiers who have confidence in their commanders, in their training, and in their weapons can face the enemy with a large degree of confidence and personal peace. Although the overall circumstances may be uncertain, they can say, "Whatever happens, I am ready! I am prepared and capable of doing my best!" In God we have the very best of commanders. He is unmatched. He has also provided us with everything we need to be properly trained for battle. We have His Word, the Bible, to teach us. We have the Holy Spirit to give us understanding and to daily work peace in our heart by birthing within us a higher level of supernatural peace. Finally, we have the weapons of spiritual armor that are part of God's heart protection plan to protect our spirit man. Not only does this armor prepare us for battle but it also helps us face the conflict with inner peace.

Paul describes the armor of our peace in Ephesians 6:10-18, encouraging us to wear it faithfully so that we can stand against the "wiles of the devil" (verse 11) and the spiritual forces of darkness. Each piece plays an important part in establishing our heart in peace and preparing us for battle.

Loins girt about with truth (verse 14). Our loins are the region of strength and procreative power. To "gird our loins" means that we are preparing to undertake difficult, tiring, and challenging work. When we charge forward in the battle between soul, flesh, mind, and heart, the truth of God gives us confidence that we are winners and that no weapon fashioned against us will stand (see Is. 54:17). We then move out in the peace of certain victory.

Breastplate of righteousness (verse 14). The breastplate of righteousness covers our heart and protects it from the devil's fiery darts of unrest, disquiet, fear, worry, anger, stress, lust, temptation—whatever satan throws at us. Righteousness— our position of right standing before God made possible in Christ—is a powerful peace weapon that satan cannot withstand. We can move forward without fear because the God of our righteousness has told us over and over again "fear not"; with the words "peace, be still" He has quieted those things that would disturb our heart.

Feet shod with the preparation of the gospel of peace (verse 15). These shoes prepare us to go into the fields of the world and sow the seeds of peace so that the harvest of righteousness may be brought in. Spiritual feet are not the same as natural feet. Our spirit man goes places in the Spirit that our natural man will never see or know. For example, while we sleep our spirit man may wrestle with evil spirits, sinful thoughts, and lustful desires that in our natural man we will never know about. We may see visions, dream dreams, or receive revelations without knowing that our spirit man was working from our heart in cooperation with the Holy Spirit.

Shield of faith (verse 16). The shield of faith not only protects us from outward attacks from the world but also protects and preserves the precious treasures we keep hidden within our spirit—things like truth, God's Word, purity, joy, and unity. When this shield is in place, satan can't get through to fill our heart with lust, fear, doubt, or unbelief.

Helmet of salvation (verse 17). A helmet offers protection for the head, the brain, and the mental faculties of reason and understanding. If our mind is not at rest, our heart and spirit can be troubled. Salvation helps us look at life and the world in a whole new light, a light of confidence and of understanding the ways of God like we never have before. Putting on the helmet of salvation allows the peace of God to manifest in our mind, heart, and spirit.

Sword of the Spirit (verse 17). The sword of the Spirit is the Word of God that cleans and protects. It cuts away the spiritual buildup that would clog the arteries of the heart of our spirit man, blocking our peace:

> *For the word of God is quick, and powerful, and sharper than any twoedged sword, piercing even to the dividing asunder of soul and spirit, and of the joints and marrow, and is a discerner of the thoughts and intents of the heart* (Hebrews 4:12).

Only the Word of God has the power to cleanse our heart. An unclean heart can never show forth peace.

As soldiers of God we must walk in the gospel of peace so that the whole armor of God can be clearly seen by all who oppose us. The peace of God allows us to take command of our surroundings and situations; it allows us to advance with confidence, power, and victory.

The Rest of God

The Word of God promises that there is a future rest for the children of God. The peace of God we have in our heart today is merely a foretaste of what that future rest will be like. According to Genesis, after God finished His creative work in six days, He rested on the seventh day. Later, when God called the nation of Israel as a people unto Himself, He offered them the opportunity to enter His rest. For Israel the "promised land" represented entering the "rest" of God. They were unable to enter, however, because of unbelief and disobedience. Except for Joshua and Caleb, the entire first generation of Israelites that came out of Egypt died in the wilderness. God had brought them to the very border of the land and was prepared to take them in, but they refused to follow. In judgment on their unbelief and disobedience, God declared that they would wander in the wilderness until all the faithless generation had died. Forty years later Joshua led a new generation into the land.

The Book of Hebrews warns us not to commit the same sin of disobedience that kept the Israelites from entering God's rest:

> *Therefore, as the Holy Spirit says: "Today, if you will hear His voice, do not **harden your hearts** as in the rebellion, in the day of trial in the wilderness"…. Beware, brethren, lest there be in any of you **an evil heart** of unbelief in departing from the living God…. Therefore, since a promise remains of entering **His***

rest, let us fear lest any of you seem to have come short
of it....There remains therefore *a rest* for the people of
God....Let us therefore be diligent to enter that rest,
lest anyone fall according to the same example of disobedience (Hebrews 3:7-8,12; 4:1,9,11 NKJ).

The ancient nation of Israel never fully entered into God's
rest because it is a spiritual rest preconditioned on faithfulness
and obedience. Israel repeatedly turned from God until He
destroyed the nation and sent the people into exile. There is a
spiritual rest yet today for the people of God.

God wants us to enter His rest. He has provided a heart
protection plan to keep our heart right before Him through
faith, pure and holy living, love, joy, and peace. The degree to
which these things are manifested in our life depends on our
faithfulness and obedience. We have peace *with* God through
faith in Jesus Christ; we gain the peace *of* God in our heart
through the presence of the Holy Spirit. The more control we
allow the Lord to have over our mind, thoughts, words, and
actions, the greater will be our peace. Let's be faithful to the
Lord so that the invitation of Jesus can become real for us:

Come to Me, all you who labor and are heavy laden,
and I will give you rest. Take My yoke upon you and
learn from Me, for I am gentle and lowly in heart, and
you will find rest for your souls. For My yoke is easy
and My burden is light (Matthew 11:28-30 NKJ).

Endnotes

1. American Heart Association, "Heart, How It Works." 15 Feb. 1999. http://www.americanheart.org/Heart_and_Stroke_A_Z_Guide/hworks/html>
2. American Heart Association, "Diastolic Dysfunction." 15 Feb 1999. <http://www.americanheart.org/Heart_and_Stroke_A_Z_Guide/dias.html>
3. James Strong, *Strong's Exhaustive Concordance of the Bible* (Peabody, MA: Hendrickson Publishers, n.d.), #G1515.
4. W.E. Vine, Merrill F. Unger, and William White, Jr. *Vine's Complete Expository Dictionary of Old and New Testament Words* (Nashville: Thomas Nelson Publishers, 1985), p. 464.
5. *Strong's*, #G5432.
6. *Strong's*, #H5564.
7. *Strong's*, #H982.
8. *Strong's*, #H5341.
9. *Strong's*, #H7965.

Chapter 8

A Powerful Heart

*But as many as received Him, to them gave He **power** to become the sons of God, even to them that believe on His name (John 1:12).*

*But ye shall receive **power**, after that the Holy Ghost is come upon you: and ye shall be witnesses unto Me both in Jerusalem, and in all Judaea, and in Samaria, and unto the uttermost part of the earth (Acts 1:8).*

The first thing that most of us do when we walk into a dark room is flip on the light switch. Instantly the darkness is scattered as electrical current heats the filament of the light bulb to a white-hot intensity. The bulb will continue to shine as long as it is connected to its power source. If the switch is turned off, the bulb will go out and darkness will overtake the room once more. A steady light requires a steady power source and a solid connection.

The Gospel of John says that Jesus Christ is the spiritual light that came into a sin-darkened world:

In Him was life; and the life was the light of men. And the light shineth in darkness; and the darkness comprehended it not....That was the true Light, which lighteth

every man that cometh into the world. He was in the
world, and the world was made by Him, and the world
knew Him not. He came unto His own, and His own
received Him not (John 1:4-5,9-11).

Later, Jesus Himself said, "I am the light of the world: he
that followeth Me shall not walk in darkness, but shall have
the light of life" (Jn. 8:12b). Nevertheless, those to whom
Jesus came to give "the light of life" rejected Him because
they preferred to remain in the darkness lest their sinful condition be fully exposed (see Jn. 3:19-20).

On the other hand, those who received and welcomed "the
light of life" received "power to become the sons of God" (Jn.
1:12). They became lights themselves, carrying the divine
power source within them. He who said, "I am the light of the
world," also said to His followers, "Ye are the light of the
world....Let your light so shine before men, that they may see
your good works, and glorify your Father which is in heaven"
(Mt. 5:14,16). Referring to all believers, Paul wrote, "Ye are all
the children of light, and the children of the day: we are not
of the night, nor of darkness" (1 Thess. 5:5), and encouraged
us to "walk as children of light" (Eph. 5:8). We who know the
Lord are spiritual lights in a dark world. Through the Holy
Spirit who dwells in us, we are connected to Jesus, our divine
power source. Why then do we so often feel powerless?

Power Failure

Even though we may often hear it or even say it, the truth
that "Christ liveth in me" (Gal. 2:20) has never become a reality in the mind of many Christians. For whatever reason,
some of us have trouble accepting the fact that the Son of God
has actually taken up residence in our heart through the Holy
Spirit. Because of my heart-focused teaching and preaching
ministry, I am known in many churches as the "heart man,"
yet many times I still am guilty of not fully recognizing the
way I should the presence of the Almighty God in my heart.

Part of the reason for this state may be that the day-by-day experience of our life seems to fall far short of the promises we read in the Bible. We read that God is our strength, but we know weakness. We read that we have victory in Christ, but we most commonly experience defeat. We read that we shall receive power, but we see no power manifested in our lives. Somewhere along the line we have suffered a spiritual power failure.

Something has interrupted the flow of God's power to our heart. The problem is certainly not with God. He never changes. James says that God is the "Father of lights, with whom is no variableness, neither shadow of turning" (Jas. 1:17b), while the Book of Hebrews proclaims that "Jesus Christ [is] the same yesterday, and today, and for ever" (Heb. 13:8). The Holy Spirit who lives in the heart of every believer is a Spirit of power (see 2 Tim. 1:7). He is a power heart connector.

Every Christian has access to the power of God. Our body is a spiritual power plant, yet too often there is little or no flow of power. Why? The outward production of any power plant is dependent upon its ability to function and produce.

Thus, the problem lies with our connection to the power source. If the contacts on an electrical switch are corroded, dirty, or broken, no power will flow to the light bulb, radio, or whatever else we are trying to use. Likewise, if our heart is dirty or corroded with impure imaginations and worldly desires, no spiritual power will be manifested in our life. Our connection to the power source can be broken through disobedience, willful sin, failure to read God's Word, failure to pray, lust, greed, envy, bitterness—in short, anything that manifests the things of the flesh rather than the things of the Spirit. We must remain vitally connected to Jesus, our power source. Otherwise we are useless. Jesus said, "I am the vine, ye are the branches: He that abideth in Me, and I in him, the same bringeth forth much fruit: for *without Me ye can do nothing*" (Jn. 15:5).

The power available to us through the Spirit is greater than any other kind of power anywhere because it is God's power.

He wants His power to be on display before the world in the heart and life of His children. Sadly, in ignorance, we the Church have not walked in His power. Today's holy Church must become a "power house" of God to counterbalance the sin and evil in the world and to clearly present the gospel of Jesus Christ to the lost. We will not be powerless if we maintain a firm power base in Christ, the living Word of God. He is both the source of our power and the channel through which it flows to us. With His power in us, our heart can stand against all unrighteousness and we can walk daily in victory.

Dynamic Duo

In order to understand God's power in our heart we need to approach it from two different perspectives, each of which is represented by a Greek word. *Dunamis* occurs 123 times in the New Testament; it means "power" in the sense of the *ability* to act or do something. Usually used in reference to miraculous power, it also means "might," "strength," "miracle," and "wonderful work."[1] Our English words *dynamic*, *dynamo*, and *dynamite* are all derived from *dunamis*. One of the most familiar uses of the word is in Jesus' promise to His disciples:

> *But ye shall receive power* [dunamis], *after that the Holy Ghost is come upon you: and ye shall be witnesses unto Me both in Jerusalem, and in all Judaea, and in Samaria, and unto the uttermost part of the earth* (Acts 1:8).

After the disciples were baptized and filled with the Holy Spirit, they had the *power* to *act;* they had a divine, supernatural *ability* to minister, preach, heal, and teach effectively in the name of Jesus that they had not had before.

Exousia, used 103 times in the New Testament, carries the idea of the *authority* to act or do something. In fact, it can be translated "authority" as well as "jurisdiction," "liberty," "right," and "delegated influence."[2] Anyone who acts under delegated authority exercises *exousia*. One familiar verse that uses this word is found early in the Gospel of John:

> *But as many as received Him, to them gave He power [exousia] to become the sons of God, even to them that believe on His name* (John 1:12).

To everyone who trusts in Him for forgiveness and salvation Jesus gives the power, the *authority*, the *right*, to become children of God. In fact, most Bible versions other than the King James use the word *right* instead of *power* in this verse. We do not possess within ourselves the *ability* to become children of God. Jesus gives us the right, however, and exercises *His* power (*dunamis*) to bring it about when we place our faith and trust in Him.

To be effective, *dunamis* and *exousia* must be exercised in conjunction with each other. Neither is complete without the other. Having the *ability* to act (*dunamis*) doesn't mean much if we do not have the *authority* to act (*exousia*). A soldier's readiness and ability to accomplish a mission mean little until he is authorized to proceed by receiving orders from his superiors. Those orders give him the *authority* to exercise his *ability*. On the other hand, authority means very little without the ability to carry it out. A soldier cannot exercise his authority to fight if he lacks the training, weapons, or other resources to do so.

As disciples of Christ we have been given both the ability (*dunamis*) to live victoriously and minister effectively in Jesus' name and the authority (*exousia*) to act as His representatives on the earth. Second Corinthians 5:18-20 says that we are ambassadors for Christ with a ministry of reconciliation: to reconcile the world with God.

A good example of the dual nature of the power given to believers is found in Luke's Gospel when Jesus was preparing to send His disciples out to preach in the surrounding villages:

> *Then He called His twelve disciples together, and gave them **power** [dunamis] and **authority** [exousia] over*

all devils, and to cure diseases. And He sent them to preach the kingdom of God, and to heal the sick (Luke 9:1-2).

Jesus gave them both the ability and the authority to act in His name. As the disciples exercised the authority Jesus had delegated to them, both demons and disease responded to their commands as they would have to Jesus Himself.

Jesus' delegation of power and authority to His disciples was an extension of the relationship in which He walked with the Father. In everything He did Jesus exercised His power (*dunamis*) within the bounds of the authority given to Him by His Father:

> ...*Verily, verily, I say unto you,* **The Son can do nothing of Himself, but what He seeth the Father do**: *for what things soever He doeth, these also doeth the Son likewise....For as the Father hath life in Himself; so hath He given to the Son to have life in Himself; and hath given Him authority to execute judgment also, because He is the Son of man....*I can of Mine own self do nothing: *as I hear, I judge: and My judgment is just; because* **I seek not Mine own will, but the will of the Father** *which hath sent Me* (John 5:19,26-27,30).

In the same manner, the only way we can have spiritual power in our lives and exercise it properly and effectively is to keep ourselves in proper relationship with Jesus, the source and supplier of our power. God cannot release in our heart more power than it can hold or use. Useless power or unused power is a shame before God. It's a dishonor to Him. Spiritual warfare is rampant; there are many battles in which we need to use our power to its full measure.

Heart Power

Part of the problem with the Church today is that far too many believers—whether due to ignorance, unbelief, or worldly living—are not using their God-given power. God has done His part. In addition to sending His Son to redeem us, give us life, and make us righteous before Him, God has given us His Word to nourish our heart and spirit, has provided nine "power gifts" through which we can reveal His power and greatness in the world, and has empowered us through the ninefold fruit of the Spirit to build up His Body, the Church, and to give testimony to the world of the truth of the gospel. Our heart must be properly connected to our divine power supply if these gifts and fruit are to manifest themselves fully in our lives. God wants His power to be displayed in His people, and His gospel to be heard by all the nations. In fact, Christ established His Church—His "Body" on earth—in order to reveal His power in the earth to all people. Every born-again believer has a new heart created by the Lord to manifest power!

Consider power in the political realm. Will Russia or China attack the United States? No. Why? We have too much power. But there are countries that live in fear due to their lack of power. In the same way, our hidden man of the heart has power with God. We should not fear; rather, we should use the power contained in the treasures God has hidden in our heart.

Christ, anointed by God with power, was our perfect example. As believers we are to be like Him, speaking as He spoke and working as He worked. The power at work in us is the same power that raised Christ from the dead. Consider Paul's words in Ephesians:

*And what is the **exceeding greatness of His power toward us** who believe, according to the working of His mighty power **which He worked in Christ when He raised Him from the dead** and seated Him at His right hand in the heavenly places* (Ephesians 1:19-20 NKJ).

The power in us is resurrection power! This resurrection power shows itself in our life through the nine spiritual gifts, or "power gifts," that all believers receive from the Holy Spirit. Paul discusses these gifts in chapter 12 of First Corinthians:

*Now concerning spiritual gifts, brethren, I do not want
you to be ignorant....There are diversities of gifts, but
the same Spirit....But the manifestation of the Spirit is
given to each one for the profit of all: for to one is given
the **word of wisdom** through the Spirit, to another the
word of knowledge through the same Spirit, to another **faith** by the same Spirit, to another **gifts of healings**
by the same Spirit, to another the working of **miracles**,
to another **prophecy**, to another **discerning of spirits**,
to another **different kinds of tongues**, to another the
interpretation of tongues. But one and the same Spirit
works all these things, distributing to each one individually as He wills (1 Corinthians 12:1,4,7-11 NKJ).*

When properly understood, recognized, and exercised in
the Church, all these gifts witness to the awesome power of
God and direct the attention of lost people toward Him. In
this way people are drawn to the truth of the gospel and are
challenged to give their heart to Christ in repentance and
faith. These same gifts enable believers to witness and minister in the power of the Spirit rather than in the power of the
flesh. It is only in the power of the Spirit that anyone truly
comes to Christ.

The power of God at work in our heart produces spiritual
fruit that nourishes us to maturity in the faith and shows the
world that Jesus is real. This fruit is in stark contrast to the
"fruit" or works of the flesh:

*Now the works of the flesh are evident, which are:
adultery, fornication, uncleanness, lewdness, idolatry,
sorcery, hatred, contentions, jealousies, outbursts of
wrath, selfish ambitions, dissensions, heresies, envy,
murders, drunkenness, revelries, and the like; of which
I tell you beforehand, just as I also told you in time
past, that those who practice such things will not
inherit the kingdom of God. But the fruit of the Spirit
is love, joy, peace, longsuffering, kindness, goodness,*

faithfulness, gentleness, self-control. Against such there is no law (Galatians 5:19-23 NKJ).

Which is more prominent in *your* life, the fruit of the Spirit or the works of the flesh? What about your church? Are the works of the flesh short-circuiting the power of God in your heart or in the ministry of your church? Fleshly thoughts and imaginations and worldly behavior trip the circuit breakers of our heart, interrupting the flow of spiritual power.

Power Up

When we become one with the Lord, we obtain awesome heart power. As we learn to walk in true holiness, the power level increases because more of our heart is available for the Spirit to use. A powerful heart is faith-powered, Word-fed, love-watered, blood-covered, and Spirit-filled. It contains God's power alive within us.

We need heart power to overcome the temptations, evil or lustful thoughts, and worldly influences that come against us all the time. So often we grieve and vex the Lord and trouble His heart when we don't take care to keep out the things that will shut off the power flow. Heart power will see us through to victory despite the many storms of life: the windy days and dark nights; the sickness, sin, and sorrow. Heart power will teach us to speak from the heart, hear with the heart, and see from the heart all things that are holy and right. It will give us the authority and the strength to stand firm in the days of trouble, even unto death.

God is calling for His Church in these last days to stand up and be counted, to move out in power against the sin, evil, and godlessness in our world. The secret to power in the Church is the fullness of God in the life of believers. For far too long the Church has ignored or neglected the power of God in her midst that is revealed in true praise and worship, in divine healing, and in supernatural deliverance that sets captives free. God's power is found in more than just preaching and teaching; it is also evident in the real manifestation of the outpouring of His Spirit. Christ in us is our hope of glory (see Col. 1:27). The important thing is not so much the work we do as it is the One who works in us. We should work in the Church as Christ works in us. Heart power will make the difference between a Church that prevails in the heat of battle and one that retreats in defeat and disarray.

It's time for the Church to *power up!*

Keep the Power Flowing

The Scriptures give us plenty of practical guidance for building and preserving spiritual power in our life. Here are some disciplines that every one of us needs to practice regularly:

1. *Continue daily in God's Word* (Ps. 119:11,105; Acts 17:11; 2 Tim. 2:15).
2. *Pray without ceasing* (Phil. 4:6; 1 Thess. 5:17).
3. *Walk by faith and not by sight* (2 Cor. 5:7).
4. *Eat clean foods and drink pure water* (Dan. 1).
5. *Maintain a righteous and holy lifestyle* (Mt. 5:6; Rom. 6:13; 1 Pet. 1:15-16).
6. *Love everyone, especially the brethren, and Christ above all* (Mk. 12:30-31; Lk. 15:26-32; Jn. 13:35; 1 Thess. 3:12; 1 Pet. 2:17).
7. *Praise and worship the Lord continually* (Ps. 96:9; 146:2; Mt. 4:10).
8. *Give your tithes and offerings faithfully* (Mal. 3:10).
9. *Keep joy alive* (Jn. 15:11; 16:24; 17:13; Rom. 15:13; Gal. 5:22).
10. *Forgive quickly those who hurt you* (Mt. 5:23-24; 6:14-15; 18:21-35).
11. *Judge yourself daily* (1 Cor. 11:31-32; 2 Cor. 13:5).
12. *Strive to live in peace with everyone* (Rom. 12:18; 1 Thess. 5:13; Jas. 3:18).
13. *Serve the Lord with all your heart* (Deut. 10:12; 1 Sam. 12:20; Ps. 100:2).

14. *Keep your hands to the gospel plow* (Ps. 126:5-6; Lk. 9:62; Gal. 6:9).
15. *Obey legitimate leadership, both Church and civil* (Rom. 13:1; Tit. 3:1; Heb. 13:17).
16. *Keep Christ as your power source and base* (Jn. 15:1-8; Gal. 2:20; 1 Jn. 2:24).
17. *Speak right words* (Eph. 4:29; Col. 4:6; Tit. 2:7-8).
18. *Think right thought patterns* (Rom. 12:1-2; 1 Cor. 2:15-16; Eph. 4:23-24; Phil. 4:8; 1 Pet. 1:13).
19. *Stay on fire, ignited by God's Word* (Jer. 20:9; 1 Cor. 9:16; 2 Tim. 4:2).
20. *Stay thirsty and hot for Christ* (Mt. 5:6; Jn. 7:37).
21. *Do good always* (Mt. 5:38-44; Lk. 6:31; Gal. 6:10; Jas. 4:17; 1 Pet. 3:11).
22. *Keep your heart open to God* (Deut. 6:5; Ps. 40:8; 51:17; 57:7; Joel 2:13).
23. *Work hard in the Church* (Gal. 6:9; 1 Cor. 15:58; Eph. 4:11-13; Heb. 10:25; Jas. 1:25).
24. *Work toward perfection (completeness and spiritual maturity)* (2 Cor. 13:11; 2 Tim. 3:16-17).

Dear saints, there is power—healing power, saving power, wonder-working power—in the name of Jesus and in the precious blood of the Lamb! Let's keep the power flowing! Calling on His name in faith releases a power in our heart that makes us more than conquerors and joint heirs with Jesus, preserved by His blood. As we learn more and more to walk in the Spirit, our heart becomes more like the heart of Christ and He gives us the strength and courage to face the challenges of the world. A powerless heart is full of fear and uncertainty. A powerful heart is free of fear. Let's take Paul's words to Timothy "to heart" as we seek to nurture and preserve the spiritual power contained in the hidden treasures of our heart:

For God hath not given us the spirit of fear; but of power, and of love, and of a sound mind (2 Timothy 1:7).

Endnotes

1. James Strong, *Strong's Exhaustive Concordance of the Bible* (Peabody, MA: Hendrickson Publishers, n.d.), #G1411.
2. *Strong's*, #G1849.

Chapter 9

A Faithful Heart

And I will betroth thee unto Me for ever; yea, I will betroth thee unto Me in righteousness, and in judgment, and in lovingkindness, and in mercies. I will even betroth thee unto Me in faithfulness: and thou shalt know the Lord (Hosea 2:19-20).

For this cause shall a man leave his father and mother, and shall be joined unto his wife, and they two shall be one flesh. This is a great mystery: but I speak concerning Christ and the church. Nevertheless let every one of you in particular so love his wife even as himself; and the wife see that she reverence her husband (Ephesians 5:31-33).

It's no secret that in recent years the institutions of marriage and the family have been under attack. Traditional concepts based on the Word of God have really taken a beating. Judging from the content of many movies, television sitcoms, and dramas we could conclude that "one-night-stands," "live-in" relationships, and extramarital affairs have become the "norm" while monogamous marriage and faithfulness between partners are relegated to the ranks of the old-fashioned and out-moded.

In our schools, prayer is out and condoms are in; virginity is mocked while teen pregnancies, births, and abortions continue to rise. Instead of learning character and responsibility, our students are taught in error that "safe sex" is the solution. Many of them come from broken homes and face serious future problems in their own relationships because they do not have a healthy, positive example to follow.

Marital infidelity is rampant. It has brought down well-known and highly respected Christian leaders and has been exposed (and rationalized) even in some of the highest offices of our land. In many quarters, adultery is assumed by the majority and suspected by the rest. Sad to say, the problem is also rampant within the Church. Married pastors run off with their secretaries, respected deacons sleep with women other than their wife, and other church members, both men and women, carry on all sorts of improper and immoral relationships. I think the situation is much more serious than we want to believe.

Whatever happened to good old faithfulness and commitment? Whatever happened to the Church setting an example *for* the world instead of being a copy *of* the world? We need to take a close, hard look at ourselves and our churches. Infidelity is a deadly heart condition that infects our human marital and sexual relationships as well as our spiritual relationships.

Infidelity is a heart problem.

Satan's Playground

Satan has had his eye on the human marriage covenant since the day Eve first came to Adam. Marriage has become one of the devil's biggest playgrounds. From his own heart, spiritually "divorced" from God because of his rebellion, satan sowed the seeds of conflict, confusion, deception, dishonor, lack of love, selfishness, adultery, and division into the fertile soil of the human heart. Sin poisoned the heart of Adam and of Eve, broke their union with God, and brought strife and hardship into their relationship with each other. Without exception, every person of every generation since has inherited these problems.

Why do so many marriages today—even Christian marriages—fail? The reasons are many: lust has replaced love, the pursuit of things has replaced the pursuit of happiness, fear has replaced passion, strife has replaced unity, selfishness has replaced self-giving, the heart is focused on the god of this world rather than on the God of the universe; the list could go on. Marriages fail because the partners do not honor and glorify God through a life of holiness and truth.

Ruptures in the relationship between husbands and wives reflect the rift between men and God. *Our marriage is not right because our heart is not right.* We are not faithful to each other because we are not faithful to God. We do not honor each other because we do not honor God. We do not submit to each other in love because we do not submit to God. Our heart is stubborn, selfish, and rebellious, and these attitudes show up in our marriage. Many unmarried people have trouble relating to members of the opposite sex for these same reasons. Many married couples leave God in their living room as they proceed to the bedroom to engage in sexual activities. Where God is not, satan may easily rule or cause problems. Without Christ in the midst of a sexual release or experience, a demon of lust may well be magnified.

The society we live in places a low value on commitment, particularly where human relationships are concerned. Men and women enter into sexual relationships, establish "live-in" arrangements, and even get married with the idea that when times get tough or when trouble comes they can simply quit. Commitment cannot be "drummed up" in the midst of a crisis; it must be established *beforehand.* An uncommitted relationship will not survive the inevitable rocky roads and slippery spots.

Faithfulness comes only from a faithful heart, and a faithful heart knows that faithfulness in marriage arises from the understanding that marriage is both a *lasting* covenant and a covenant of *love*.

A Lasting Covenant

From the very beginning God created man for faithfulness in relationships. God is faithful by nature, and the humans created in His image were to be faithful as well. Man was to be faithful to God above all, and from this would flow faithfulness in every other relationship. When God placed Adam in the garden of Eden, He established the parameters of a relationship based on love, trust, and faithfulness:

> *And the Lord God commanded the man, saying, Of every tree of the garden thou mayest freely eat: but of the tree of the knowledge of good and evil, thou shalt not eat of it: for in the day that thou eatest thereof thou shalt surely die* (Genesis 2:16-17).

Adam would demonstrate his trust and love for God by his faithful obedience.

Faithfulness extended to human relationships as well. After God made woman from Adam's side, Adam declared in delight that she was "bone of my bones, and flesh of my flesh" (Gen. 2:23). The next verse reveals God's desire and intention for the relationship between the man and the woman: "Therefore shall a man leave his father and his mother, and shall cleave unto his wife: and they shall be one flesh" (Gen. 2:24). God ordained faithfulness and commitment between husband and wife from the very start.

Throughout the Bible God's relationship with His people is pictured as a marriage covenant. The first of the Ten Commandments, "Thou shalt have no other gods before Me" (Ex. 20:3), is a call to faithfulness. God is revealed as the "husband" of His people: "For *thy Maker is thine husband*; the Lord of hosts is His name; and thy Redeemer the Holy One of Israel;

the God of the whole earth shall He be called" (Is. 54:5). In the New Testament, Christ is the Bridegroom (see Mt. 25:1-13; Jn. 3:28-29), and the Church is the Bride of Christ (see Rev. 21:2,9-10). Disobedience on the part of God's people, particularly turning their heart away from God, is regarded as spiritual adultery:

> I was crushed by their **adulterous heart** which has departed from Me, and by their eyes which play the harlot after their idols; they will loathe themselves for the evils which they committed in all their abominations (Ezekiel 6:9b NKJ).

The Scriptures also make it clear that God's purpose is for the marriage covenant to be a *lasting* relationship. The spiritual union between God and His people is *eternal* in nature:

> And I **will betroth thee unto Me for ever**; yea, I will betroth thee unto Me in **righteousness**, and in **judgment**, and in **lovingkindness**, and in **mercies**. I will even betroth thee unto Me in **faithfulness**: and **thou shalt know the Lord** (Hosea 2:19-20).

The Hebrew word translated "know" in verse 20 is *yada* and is the same word found in Genesis 4:1: "And Adam *knew* Eve his wife...." *Yada* as used in the Old Testament "expresses a multitude of shades of knowledge gained by the senses... God's knowledge of man...man's knowledge...acquaintance with a person...sexual intercourse...one's relation to the divine."[1] In the context of these verses the emphasis seems to be more on the *intimacy* of the knowledge rather than on the nature of it; it is a knowledge gained from face-to-face contact or firsthand experience.

Likewise, human marriage is intended to be a lifelong relationship between one husband and one wife. When it does not work out that way, the problem lies not with God's plan but with the heart of man. Jesus made this clear one day when the Pharisees sought to trap Him with a question about divorce:

And He answered and said unto them, Have ye not read, that He which made them at the beginning made them male and female, and said, For this cause shall a man leave father and mother, and shall cleave to his wife: and they twain shall be one flesh? Wherefore they are no more twain, but one flesh. **What therefore God hath joined together, let not man put asunder.** *They say unto Him, Why did Moses then command to give a writing of divorcement, and to put her away? He saith unto them,* **Moses because of the hardness of your hearts suffered you to put away your wives: but from the beginning it was not so** (Matthew 19:4-8).

God commands and expects faithfulness in the marriage covenant between husband and wife because human marriage is a symbol, a type, or a picture of the spiritual union between God and His people, and between Christ and His Church. The same God who said, "Thou shalt have no other gods before Me," also said, "Thou shalt not commit adultery" (Ex. 20:3,14). Faithfulness to both of these commandments (and to all the others) comes from a faithful heart firmly established in a covenant of love.

A Love Covenant

Christian marriage is a love covenant involving a *total commitment* of the mind and heart of a man and a woman; it is a permanent oneness of two persons joined together according to the operation and desire of God's own heart. The result of an inward work of the Holy Spirit, it is a lifelong contract uniting eye to eye, mind to mind, body to body, spirit to spirit, and heart to heart. It calls for mutual submission of body, spirit, and will to each other and to God. Christian marriage is a *three-way* love relationship between a husband, a wife, and Jesus Christ. Paul described the proper relationship this way:

Wives, submit yourselves unto your own husbands, as unto the Lord....Husbands, love your wives, even as Christ also loved the church, and gave Himself for it...For this cause shall a man leave his father and mother, and shall be joined unto his wife, and they two shall be one flesh. This is a great mystery: but I speak concerning Christ and the church. Nevertheless let every one of you in particular so love his wife even as himself; and the wife see that she reverence her husband (Ephesians 5:22,25,31-33).

Biblical marriage is mutual self-sacrificing love and submission between a husband and wife under the lordship of Jesus Christ; it is a oneness of three hearts, with the human couple being joined together in the heart of God. It is not a one-time event as much as it is a growing process; it is not something two people *do* as much as something they *become* over time as the Lord builds the relationship in their heart. It only takes a few minutes to "get married"; it takes a *lifetime* to build a marriage.

This love covenant begins with the love of God sown in our heart by the Holy Spirit through faith. God directs the paths of His children, both men and women, and brings couples together according to His will. He causes His love to bloom in their heart toward each other. As their love grows, so does the desire to commit themselves to each other for life in the holy bond of marriage. Such commitment takes time to develop. It does not happen overnight. Is marriage of the flesh or of the Spirit? Can the problem for believers be that many get married in the flesh, but remain separated in the Spirit?

Christian marriage provides provides an outlet for the mutual expression of selfless *agape* for love, for procreation, and for precious friendship and companionship, and shows the world a model of the relationships that exist in Heaven between the three persons of the Trinity and between God and humanity. Christian marriage also provides a training ground to prepare us for living and reigning for all eternity with Christ, our Bridegroom.

The growth and development of this divine marriage covenant, both physical and spiritual, can be understood better perhaps by examining it from three stages: courtship, engagement, and wedding. I want to make it clear that the discussion that follows refers specifically to *Christian* men and women entering into relationships.

Courtship

Most marriages (at least in the western world) begin with a period of courtship during which the couple gets to know each other and a friendship blossoms. As the relationship grows they realize that they love each other and want to spend the rest of their life together. The man (usually) proposes marriage, the woman accepts, and the couple becomes engaged. During the period of engagement they continue to grow in their love and understanding. The marriage itself commences with the wedding ceremony, after which the newlyweds embark on a lifetime of marital bliss and joy (at least that's the ideal and dream of most couples). Unfortunately, many times it doesn't work out that way.

The early period of courtship and friendship is very important to the prospect of marital success and happiness. It is during this time that a couple dates and talks and begins to learn and understand each other's heart, desires, and dreams, as well as each other's personality, attitude, and purpose in life. God begins to unite the heart of the couple during the courtship period. His love is planted in their heart, and their mutual faith in Christ helps them settle into a strong friendship with each other. Their commitment to Christ also helps them keep their thoughts and heart pure and to remain sexually abstinent.

Even a friendship involves commitment. The couple must set their heart to be friends and commit themselves to the relationship. They must also commit their relationship to God and pledge to be faithful to His standards of morality and purity. Even at this early stage of the relationship it is very important to stay alert because satan always stands ready to trip up Christian couples by putting impure, immoral, or jealous thoughts in their mind or by trying to stir up lust, thus gaining an early foothold in their heart and mind. This is a time for the Christian friends to talk about spiritual matters and to pray together regularly. Prayer fertilizes the relationship, nourishing the seeds of love, trust, and unity that the Lord has planted. Watered by commitment and strengthened by mutual submission, love then comes alive. A Spirit-led period of courtship then leads to the next level, when the couple commits to engagement in anticipation of marriage.

From the perspective of the divine marriage covenant between Christ and His Church, the courtship period could be likened to the time Jesus spent calling and teaching His disciples. As they followed Him and got to know Him, their love for Him grew and their understanding increased concerning who He was. Jesus shared His love with them and they built strong friendships. The disciples learned to think and act like Jesus and eventually, except for Judas Iscariot, committed their life to Jesus and accepted Him as Savior and Lord. It was at this point of personal decision that the "courtship" period ended and the "engagement" period began. In the case of Judas, he broke off the relationship when he rejected and betrayed Jesus.

Every one of us who comes into contact with Jesus goes through a similar process. He courts us, wanting to enter into a relationship with us. He wants to be our friend and to deliver us from our sin. Whether or not this budding relationship moves beyond the courtship phase is up to us. We must decide, as the disciples did, whether or not to believe and receive Jesus. His invitation is open. The choice is ours.

Engagement

In biblical days the period of engagement was more binding than it is in our society. As with a marriage itself, an engagement could be broken only by divorce. One reason for this is that marriages in those days typically were arranged— sometimes years in advance—by the parents of the engaged couple. An engaged couple was considered married in all respects except that there had not yet been a wedding ceremony and they did not live together or have sexual relations.

This is why Joseph faced a dilemma in his heart and mind when he learned that Mary was pregnant with Christ. Because Mary was pledged to him, Joseph had the right under the law to have her stoned. Because he was a man who honored God and loved Mary, he sought to divorce her quietly. It took a visit from an angel for Joseph to understand, lay aside his questions and doubts, and complete his marriage to Mary.

For Christian couples, the engagement period is a time to stay in unity with God's will, to listen faithfully to His voice, to obey His Word, and to seek to be led by the Spirit of God in every aspect of the relationship. There is great pleasure, joy, and excitement just in being in each other's company. The engagement ring is given and received as a pledge of love and exclusive commitment to one another in a faithful, lifelong relationship. Much joy and anticipation are shared as wedding plans are made. As the day approaches, anticipation grows and with it stronger emotions and sexual desire. The danger of slipping into sexual sin increases as well, because satan is always watching for an opportunity to enter the relationship. Engaged Christian couples must be even more thoroughly committed during this time to purity and holiness, and to being one in action, heart, and soul under Christ's leadership.

The engagement period is a time for Christian couples to make serious preparation, putting on the whole armor of God and fighting the good fight of faith for purity, holiness, and faithfulness both to Christ and to each other. Mutual commitment and respect should grow even stronger and the couple should spend regular time together in prayer and Bible study. A successful engagement (and marriage) requires that the couple keep Christ as the focal point of everything. The Lord will bring the victory.

Concerning the divine marriage covenant, Christ is the Bridegroom and His Church is His Bride. Everyone who receives Jesus as Savior and Lord enters into the divine "engagement" with Christ and becomes a member of the bridal company of the Lamb. The Church on earth between Christ's ascension and His return is the Church in her divine "engagement period." It is a time for faithful living, obedient work, and tireless ministry out of love for our Bridegroom, for whom we watch with confident and joyful anticipation of His arrival to receive us, His Bride, holy and without spot or blemish. Christ has given us the Holy Spirit as His pledge—as His "engagement ring," so to speak—that He will bring the relationship to full consummation and completion.

The Wedding

Finally, the big day arrives! After months of talking, sharing, praying, and planning, the engaged couple comes together before God and a company of witnesses to publicly proclaim their love and pledge their faithfulness and devotion to each other in the wedding ceremony. The joyous life of oneness, intimacy, and companionship they have anticipated for so long finally begins! Their hearts, their minds, and their spirits become one as they establish a brand-new home and family with Christ as the Head. The joy of sexual consummation is at hand and the happy prospects of children and a lifetime of deepening love, intimacy, and fulfillment lie ahead. There will be some rocks in the road and bumps along the way, but for the Christian husband and wife committed to the lordship of Christ in their life, home, and marriage, the best days are yet to come!

Someday Christ, the Bridegroom, will return for His Bride, His Church. He has given Himself for her to cleanse her from the stain of sin that she may be prepared as "a glorious church, not having spot, or wrinkle...holy and without blemish" (Eph. 5:27). John describes her as "the holy city, new Jerusalem, coming down from God out of heaven, prepared as a bride adorned for her husband" (Rev. 21:2). Our Bridegroom is looking for a Bride who has been pure, holy, obedient, and faithful to Him. He will come to receive her unto Himself. We who are part of that great bridal company will enter into the joy of the marriage supper of the Lamb (see Rev. 19:9). For the faithful Bride of Christ, the prospect is an eternity of joy and fulfillment in intimate fellowship with Christ, reigning with Him as joint-heirs of the Kingdom of God.

As Christians, we are called to be faithful, both in our commitment to Christ and in our human relationships. Faithfulness in marriage means that we are to be totally given over to our spouse—body, mind, and spirit—in a oneness of heart under Christ's direction. "Forsaking all others," we bend our attention to the physical, spiritual, and emotional fulfillment and well-being of the one to whom we have committed ourselves for life. This is the godly way. This is the pattern of Heaven. Unmarried believers entering into relationships with members of the opposite sex should render to each other the same honor, dignity, and respect that you would want someone to show to your future husband or wife.

Jesus said that no one can serve two masters. His call is an exclusive call. Following Christ requires that we give up all other allegiances and loyalties. His claim must take first place in our life, even over our family relationships. However, when our heart is faithful and in right relationship to Christ, He will work in us and bring all our other relationships into proper order. Faithfulness to Christ will build faithfulness in all our human relationships.

Endnote

1. R. Laird Harris, Gleason L. Archer, Jr., and Bruce K.
Waltke, eds. *Theological Wordbook of the Old Testament*
(Chicago: Moody Press, 1980), 1:366, know (#848).

Chapter 10

A Victorious Heart

But thanks be to God, which giveth us the victory through our Lord Jesus Christ (1 Corinthians 15:57).

For whatsoever is born of God overcometh the world: and this is the victory that overcometh the world, even our faith. Who is he that overcometh the world, but he that believeth that Jesus is the Son of God? (1 John 5:4-5)

Ask, and it shall be given you; seek, and ye shall find; knock, and it shall be opened unto you: for every one that asketh receiveth; and he that seeketh findeth; and to him that knocketh it shall be opened (Matthew 7:7-8).

Years ago a popular network television weekly sports program always began with the words, "The thrill of victory and the agony of defeat." Dear brothers and sisters in Christ, I hope that by now you have begun to catch the scent of victory in the air. Jesus Christ has won! The Son of God is our champion! Satan is writhing in agony over his defeat! The future is bright for the children of the Kingdom!

We who know the Lord have a sure hope of glory. But we don't have to wait until we reach Heaven to begin experiencing victory; it can be ours now, on a day-by-day basis. The Spirit of the living God has brought to life in each of us "the hidden man of the heart, in that which is not corruptible, even the ornament of a meek and quiet spirit, which is in the sight of God of great price" (1 Pet. 3:4). He has given us a new heart and placed us under His heart protection plan, strengthening our hidden man and calling forth the hidden treasures of faith, purity, love, joy, peace, power, and faithfulness. We experience these in increasing measure as we learn to submit ourselves in obedience to His will and surrender our heart to His control.

Our "hidden man of the heart" enjoys victory whenever we tap into the heart and will of God. The Lord has given us two primary ways to do this. One is through His Word. The Bible reveals everything we need to know God, to grow in Him, and to live the life of the redeemed children He saved us to be. The other resource for knowing the heart of God is prayer. Thus our daily victory depends on our faithfully studying God's Word and putting its truth into action in our life. Victory also depends on a committed life of prayer.

Gateway to God's Heart

Prayer opens the door to the heart of God and gives us direct access to all the resources of Heaven to use for His glory. The words we say and the posture we assume in prayer are not nearly as important as the attitude and condition of our heart. Remember that God does not look on outward appearance, but on the heart (see 1 Sam. 16:7). Whenever we come to a time of prayer we each need to first ask ourselves, "Is my heart right?" Words mean nothing if our heart is wrong. God spoke to Isaiah a word of judgment on His people when He said, "...this people draw near Me with their mouth, and with their lips do honour Me, but have removed their heart far from Me, and their fear toward Me is taught by the precept of men" (Is. 29:13). Unconfessed sin in our life hinders our prayers as well: "If I regard iniquity in my heart, the Lord will not hear me" (Ps. 66:18).

When our heart is clean and right before God, our prayers find a clear and open channel through which God's love, power, and resources flow. Prayer strengthens and molds our heart, bringing us into closer fellowship and oneness with God. Heart prayer builds us up so that our spirit man can obey God, giving us the power we need to do the work God has called us to do. The key to heart prayer is to pray in the will of God according to the Word of God from a heart attuned to God. How can an imperfect body (vessel) pray a perfect prayer? By praying in tongues from a perfect heart within the hidden man of the heart.

Heart prayer makes it possible for us to enter into the very presence of God. Christ opened the way for us so that we may "come boldly unto the throne of grace...obtain mercy, and find grace to help in time of need" (Heb. 4:16). We should take time to praise and worship the Lord until His presence surrounds and fills us. Confession of personal sin is always important because it removes the dirt and clutter that keeps God from speaking to us. The Bible is an excellent prayer guide, providing many verses we can meditate on and many others that express the deepest cries of our heart. Persistent prayer from a pure and clean heart that confesses His Word and is accompanied by specific requests made in faith reaches into God's heart and moves Him to respond.

Prayer is our personal time with God. It builds hedges of protection around our heart. We should therefore pray with sincerity, confidence, and expectation. Heart prayer helps magnify the anointing on our life and brings us into oneness with God. There is victory in prayer from the heart.

Theology or "Knee-ology"?

I believe that often we have too much theology and not enough "knee-ology." We satisfy ourselves with knowing the Bible, yet spend little time on our knees praying to the One who inspired it. We pride ourselves on our correct doctrine yet do not learn through prayer how to apply it in our life. We know all *about* God yet do not really *know* God in close fellowship because we don't spend much time with Him in prayer.

Don't get me wrong. Theology and doctrine are important. So is biblical knowledge. However, they have little practical value for us if we don't know how to apply them in our life. That's where prayer comes in. We need balance. Study brings us knowledge and insight, but *victory is won in the prayer closet.* For example, Daniel was delivered from the lions' mouths because he had *already* won the victory in prayer. Daniel had a long-established habit of praying to God three times a day. He knew God and enjoyed intimate fellowship with Him. There was no need for Daniel to try to get "prayed up" suddenly when crisis came. Long before the lions' den, Daniel had set his heart toward God. When he was thrown to the lions, Daniel knew that, live or die, he belonged to God. His heart was at peace and confident of victory. God responded and protected Daniel from the lions (see Dan. 6).

Three of Daniel's friends had a similar experience. Shadrach, Meshach, and Abednego refused to worship the king's idol even though, by royal decree, such refusal meant death in the fiery furnace. These three young Hebrew men were men of prayer, however, and their heart and spirit were devoted totally to God. When the crisis came, they were ready. Because they remained faithful to God, He delivered them. The Lord protected them so that neither they nor their clothing burned. He also met them face to face and walked with them in the midst of the fire. Shadrach, Meshach, and Abednego won the victory *in advance* because they were devoted men of prayer (see Dan. 3). It's past time that the Church teach its members that a clean heart assures us of the victory and that a right walk with God gives us the victory in advance.

Even our Lord Himself achieved victory through prayer. The four Gospels clearly indicate that Jesus prayed regularly to His Father. Several times we are told that He rose during the night and went to a solitary place to pray, or that He prayed all night before making a major decision (such as choosing the 12 men who would be His closest associates). When facing His greatest crisis, His approaching death, Jesus again turned to prayer. He agonized in the garden of Gethsemane to the point of sweating drops of blood. His communion with the Father gave Jesus the strength and resolve to face the cross and fulfill His Father's will and purpose. Prayer carried Jesus through the crisis and on to victory. If Jesus' victory depended on prayer, how much more, then, does ours!

Let us not neglect reading and studying the Bible or listening to anointed preaching and teaching. Let us be careful to examine our doctrines and beliefs against Scripture to make sure they are correct. All this is important. However, let us make *absolutely* sure that we do not neglect prayer. This is where the true secret of our victory lies. Prayer changes things. It hinders sin, allows us to enjoy God's favor, and strengthens every area of our life. It increases our faith, molds and conditions our heart, and brings our entire being—body, soul, and spirit—under the control of Christ.

Praying in the Spirit

One of the most controversial and least understood areas of prayer for many believers and churches is "praying in the Spirit," or praying in tongues. Many denominations are suspicious of tongues; some condemn tongues outright. This is an unfortunate and puzzling position because the attitude of the New Testament is so different! In his first Letter to the Corinthians Paul wrote, "Wherefore, brethren, covet to prophesy, and *forbid not to speak with tongues.* Let all things be

done decently and in order" (1 Cor. 14:39-40). Part of the reason Paul wrote to the Corinthians was to correct the church's
abuse of spiritual gifts, particularly tongues. Apparently, the
practice of speaking in tongues had gotten out of control in
Corinth with the result that the church's witness was being
damaged. Paul's instructions were intended to restore decency
and order, not by banning speaking in tongues but by returning it to its proper role.

All the spiritual gifts, when exercised in a church, should
serve to edify or build up the Body of Christ. When accompanied by the gift of interpretation, speaking in tongues edifies
the church because everyone present can benefit from the mes-
sage. Privately, tongues is a wonderful and marvelous gift. It is
a special, God-ordained prayer language in which our spirit,
through the Holy Spirit, communicates directly with the heart
of God in a way no other language can. Speaking and praying
in tongues must come forth from the heart, and then it sur-
passes all known language and prayer with understanding.

When satan hears us pray, he tries to distract us, to cloud
our mind with other things, or in many other ways to hinder
us. However, he cannot understand the language of praying in
the Spirit. Since he cannot understand it, he cannot distort or
hinder it. Spirit prayer flows directly from our heart to God's
heart. Without the Spirit, we cannot know the heart or mind
of God. The Spirit knows, however, and prays in us and for us
accordingly. In his Letter to the Romans Paul wrote:

> *Likewise the Spirit also helpeth our infirmities:* **for we**
> **know not what we should pray for as we ought: but**
> **the Spirit itself maketh intercession for us with**
> **groanings which cannot be uttered.** *And He that*
> *searcheth the hearts knoweth what is the mind of the*
> *Spirit, because He maketh intercession for the saints*
> *according to the will of God* (Romans 8:26-27).

In any given situation, and especially when we don't know
how to pray or what to pray, praying in tongues is the best way

to pray. It stops satan in his tracks and builds us up in our individual life as believers, putting us in a sound place in God and opening up the fullness of His power and divine resources. One of the reasons praying in tongues is so effective is that it is not hindered by the impurities and weaknesses of our sinful human nature. Instead of our imperfect heart trying to touch the perfect heart of God, praying in the Spirit allows the perfect heart of the Spirit to touch the perfect heart of God on our behalf. Praying in the Spirit is a gift from God that bypasses man's intellect, reasoning, wisdom, flesh, and understanding, reaching directly from spirit to Spirit, heart to Heart, and mind to Mind.

He who trusts his own heart is foolish. In the Spirit we pray to a God whom we see not, from a heart we know not, for a problem or situation, knowing by faith that it is done. Praying in the Spirit is better for the heart than praying in English. Although God hears both, prayers in English soothe the mind and emotions, whereas prayers of the Spirit soothe the heart and soul.

Patterns for Prayer

The Gospels record two particular prayers of Jesus that are instructive to us in learning how to pray. One, found in Matthew and Luke, is known both as the "Lord's Prayer" and the "Model Prayer," while the second, found in John, is often called the "High Priestly Prayer." Matthew includes the Lord's Prayer as part of Jesus' Sermon on the Mount:

After this manner therefore pray ye: Our Father which art in heaven, Hallowed be Thy name. Thy kingdom come. Thy will be done in earth, as it is in heaven. Give us this day our daily bread. And forgive us our debts, as we forgive our debtors. And lead us not into temptation, but deliver us from evil: For Thine is the kingdom, and the power, and the glory, for ever. Amen (Matthew 6:9-13).

This "model" prayer follows Jesus' teaching about the proper attitude and spirit of prayer. God-pleasing prayer does not aim at gaining the attention of men, nor does it necessarily involve a lot of words. Jesus' prayer here contains only 66 words, yet provides a perfect pattern for meaningful prayer. Effective prayer is focused on God and is plain, simple, direct, and to the point. Jesus' prayer is all of these. It contains praise, humble submission to God's will, dependence on God for daily care and the necessities of life, giving and receiving forgiveness, and recognition of God's absolute sovereignty.

The "High Priestly Prayer" is found in chapter 17 of John and is both a beautiful example of intercessory prayer and a revealing look at the heart of Jesus:

> *I have manifested Thy name unto the men which Thou gavest Me out of the world: Thine they were, and Thou gavest them Me; and they have kept Thy word....I pray for them: I pray not for the world, but for them which Thou hast given Me; for they are Thine....and I am glorified in them....keep through Thine own name those whom Thou hast given Me, that they may be one, as We are....that they might have My joy fulfilled in themselves....I pray not that Thou shouldest take them out of the world, but that Thou shouldest keep them from the evil....Sanctify them through Thy truth: Thy word is truth....Neither pray I for these alone, but for them also which shall believe on Me through their word...And the glory which Thou gavest Me I have given them; that they may be one, even as We are one* (John 17:6,9-11,13,15,17,20,22).

Intercessory prayer is "standing in the gap" for other people; it is praying to God on behalf of others. Throughout this prayer shines the love of Jesus for His disciples, those who walked with Him in Palestine as well as "them also which shall believe on Me through their word," a group that includes all of us who know Jesus today. This prayer teaches us that God honors and loves unselfish prayers raised on behalf of the good and needs of other people.

Both the Lord's Prayer and the High Priestly Prayer provide examples and guidelines for us in learning how to pray in a manner and spirit that align our heart with the heart of God.

Elements of Effective Prayer

Effective, victorious, prevailing prayer is heart prayer—prayer that is Spirit-fed and Spirit-led from our heart to God's heart. God's Word provides instruction on the elements that make up God-pleasing, God-moving prayer.

1. *Pray in Jesus' name*: "And whatsoever ye shall ask in My name, that will I do, that the Father may be glorified in the Son. If ye shall ask any thing in My name, I will do it" (Jn. 14:13-14).

2. *Pray from pure motives*: "Ye have not, because ye ask not. Ye ask, and receive not, because ye ask amiss, that ye may consume it upon your lusts" (Jas. 4:2b-3).

3. *Pray in faith*: "If ye have faith as a grain of mustard seed, ye shall say unto this mountain, Remove hence to yonder place; and it shall remove; and nothing shall be impossible unto you" (Mt. 17:20b).

4. *Pray with boldness*: "Seeing then that we have a great high priest, that is passed into the heavens, Jesus the Son of God, let us hold fast our profession....Let us therefore come boldly unto the throne of grace, that we may obtain mercy, and find grace to help in time of need" (Heb. 4:14,16).

5. *Pray according to God's will*: "And this is the confidence that we have in Him, that, if we ask any thing according to His will, He heareth us: and if we know that He hear us, whatsoever we ask, we know that we have the petitions that we desired of Him" (1 Jn. 5:14-15).

6. *Pray with a pure heart*: "If I regard iniquity in my heart, the Lord will not hear me: but verily God hath heard me; He hath attended to the voice of my prayer" (Ps. 66:18-19).

7. *Pray with a humble heart:* "If My people, which are called by My name, shall humble themselves, and pray, and seek My face, and turn from their wicked ways; then will I hear from heaven, and will forgive their sin, and will heal their land" (2 Chron. 7:14).

8. *Pray with persistence:* "Ask, and it shall be given you; seek, and ye shall find; knock, and it shall be opened unto you: for every one that asketh receiveth; and he that seeketh findeth; and to him that knocketh it shall be opened" (Mt. 7:7-8); "Pray without ceasing" (1 Thess. 5:17).

9. *Pray with a forgiving spirit:* "And when ye stand praying, forgive, if ye have ought against any: that your Father also which is in heaven may forgive you your trespasses. But if ye do not forgive, neither will your Father which is in heaven forgive your trespasses" (Mk. 11:25-26).

10. *Pray with a thankful heart:* "Be careful for nothing; but in every thing by prayer and supplication with thanksgiving let your requests be made known unto God" (Phil. 4:6).

Victory Assured

When our heart is full of the characteristics listed above, our prayers will be powerful and effective. We can expect God to do great things, things that only He can do, because we have the confidence and strength of heart to pray for great things. The only way to develop these characteristics and that level of confidence is to spend a lot of time in God's presence. *An effective, victorious prayer life takes time to develop.*

God's purpose is to grow us into the likeness of His Son. Growth always involves both joy and sadness, pleasure and pain. For this reason we all can expect to go through trials and troubles in life that only prayer will help. This builds both faith and character. Peter wrote:

Wherein ye greatly rejoice, though now for a season, if need be, ye are in heaviness through manifold temptations: that the trial of your faith, being much more precious than of gold that perisheth, though it be tried

with fire, might be found unto praise and honour and
glory at the appearing of Jesus Christ: whom having
not seen, ye love; in whom, though now ye see Him
not, yet believing, ye rejoice with joy unspeakable and
full of glory: receiving the end of your faith, even the
salvation of your souls (1 Peter 1:6-9).

No true warrior fighting the good fight of faith will emerge
without wounds or scars. In this life we will experience hurt,
pain, fear, heartache, and sorrow. However, heart prayer is a
soothing balm that cleanses and heals. It gives us the assurance of knowing that everything will be okay because,
whether we live or die, we belong to the Lord.

Victory is assured for every child of God. Nothing can
compare with the comprehensive coverage we receive under
God's heart protection plan. He is always at work in us mold-
ing, shaping, and conditioning our heart into the likeness of
His own. But God can do only as much as we allow Him to
do. Ultimately, we are responsible for how far we go in the
Lord. None of us can rise any higher than the level of our
heart. *Our heart condition determines our eternal position.*

What's the condition of your heart? When God looks at
you, what does He see? A sick, sinful heart of flesh, or a
vibrant and alive heart filled with His treasures, incorruptible
and of great value to Him? Do you present to the Lord a
believing, pure, loving, joyful, peaceful, powerful, faithful,
prayerful, and victorious heart? These are the things that God
gives as a free gift. These are the treasures that Jesus died to
provide for us. Let us look again at David's heart. Let us clearly see the heart of Abraham, Isaac, Peter, and Paul. But most
of all, let us feast our mind and heart on the heart of the Great
Physician, our "heart doctor," the Lord Jesus Christ.

Dear brothers and sisters, look deep into your heart and
ask God to do the same. Open your heart to Him and let Him
apply the balm of His grace and the medicine of His forgiveness, cleansing and transforming your heart into a vessel fit for

Heaven and the hidden treasures of the Holy Spirit. Then someday we can walk together on those streets of gold, not in sin-stained flesh, but as holy children of the King, for that is who we really are. We are men and women with hidden treasures of the heart!

For more information about the author or Heart to Heart Ministries, write to:

Heart to Heart Ministries
P.O. Box 935
Oxon Hill, MD 20750

Also available from Heart to Heart Ministries
"Fix My Heart" Gospel CD
By Bishop Donald R. Downing

Good to Me, Pride, Fix My Heart, Full Supply, Gospel Stuff, Cover Me, The Backslider, Can't You Feel His Love?, Little by Little, Full Supply (instrumental), *Shocking, Gospel Stuff*

Other
Destiny Image titles
you will enjoy reading

E*xciting titles*
by Tommy Tenney

GOD'S FAVORITE HOUSE
The burning desire of your heart can be fulfilled. God is looking for people just like you. He is a Lover in search of a people who will love Him in return. He is far more interested in you than He is interested in a building. He would hush all of Heaven's hosts to listen to your voice raised in heartfelt love songs to Him. This book will show you how to build a house of worship within, fulfilling your heart's desire and His!
ISBN 0-7684-2043-1

THE GOD CHASERS (Best-selling **Destiny Image** book)
There are those so hungry, so desperate for His presence, that they become consumed with finding Him. Their longing for Him moves them to do what they would otherwise never do: Chase God. But what does it really mean to chase God? Can He be "caught"? Is there an end to the thirsting of man's soul for Him? Meet Tommy Tenney—God chaser. Join him in his search for God. Follow him as he ignores the maze of religious tradition and finds himself, not chasing God, but to his utter amazement, caught by the One he had chased.
ISBN 0-7684-2016-4

GOD CHASERS DAILY MEDITATION
& PERSONAL JOURNAL
Does your heart yearn to have an intimate relationship with your Lord? Perhaps you long to draw closer to your heavenly Father, but you don't know how or where to start. This *Daily Meditation & Personal Journal* will help you begin a journey that will change your life. As you read and journal, you'll find your spirit running to meet Him with a desire and fervor you've never before experienced. Let your heart hunger propel you into the chase of your life...after God!
ISBN 0-7684-2040-7

Available at your local Christian bookstore.
Internet: http://www.reapernet.com

When your heart is yearning for more of Jesus, these books by Don Nori will help!

NO MORE SOUR GRAPES

Who among us wants our children to be free from the struggles we have had to bear? Who among us wants the lives of our children to be full of victory and love for their Lord? Who among us wants the hard-earned lessons from our lives given freely to our children? All these are not only possible, they are also God's will. You can be one of those who share the excitement and joy of seeing your children step into the destiny God has for them. If you answered "yes" to these questions, the pages of this book are full of hope and help for you and others just like you.
ISBN 0-7684-2037-7

THE POWER OF BROKENNESS

Accepting Brokenness is a must for becoming a true vessel of the Lord, and is a stepping-stone to revival in our hearts, our homes, and our churches. Brokenness alone brings us to the wonderful revelation of how deep and great our Lord's mercy really is. Join this companion who leads us through the darkest of nights. Discover the *Power of Brokenness*.
ISBN 1-56043-178-4

THE ANGEL AND THE JUDGMENT

Few understand the power of our judgments—or the aftermath of the words we speak in thoughtless, emotional pain. In this powerful story about a preacher and an angel, you'll see how the heavens respond and how the earth is changed by the words we utter in secret.
ISBN 1-56043-154-7

HIS MANIFEST PRESENCE

This is a passionate look at God's desire for a people with whom He can have intimate fellowship. Not simply a book on worship, it faces our triumphs as well as our sorrows in relation to God's plan for a dwelling place that is splendid in holiness and love.
ISBN 0-914903-48-9
Also available in Spanish.
ISBN 1-56043-079-6

SECRETS OF THE MOST HOLY PLACE

Here is a prophetic parable you will read again and again. The winds of God are blowing, drawing you to His Life within the Veil of the Most Holy Place. There you begin to see as you experience a depth of relationship your heart has yearned for. This book is a living, dynamic experience with God!
ISBN 1-56043-076-1

HOW TO FIND GOD'S LOVE

Here is a heartwarming story about three people who tell their stories of tragedy, fear, and disease, and how God showed them His love in a real way.
ISBN 0-914903-28-4
Also available in Spanish.
ISBN 1-56043-024-9

Available at your local Christian bookstore.

Internet: http://www.reapernet.com